Seaside
Chapel

A Contemporary Christian
Romance

Evelyn Grace

THREE STRANDS

Three Strands Publishing, LLC

Three Strands Publishing, LLC
Livermore Falls, ME 04254

Trade Paperback 978-1-7345735-7-2

Cover design: Designs by Cind designsbycind@yahoo.com
Author photo: © Click and Capture Photography

For my aunt -
Diane McLaughlin

Thank you for always being there for me.
Some of my favorite memories include you.

Contents

Chapter 1

♥

P eter Grant bit back a shout of pain as he waved his smashed thumb.

His brother was the handyman, not him. Yes, he could frame out a window. Yes, he could even build a deck. Heck, he could rewire an entire structure. He had the skills to build a house from scratch. Just like all his siblings. His father had made sure every child under his care had been able to do those things.

But Peter hadn't used many of those skills in the last few years. As a pastor, he didn't have much time for framing anything but a sermon. He used his hands to craft words, not buildings.

Peter stood and surveyed the chaos around him. The wall between what used to be the living and kitchen spaces had been reduced to studs. Wires stuck out every which way. It looked like some type of alien with long tentacles searching, waiting to grab an unsuspecting person walking by.

Drew, his handyman brother who did this type of thing for a living, was near the front window discussing something with Kate, his new wife of six weeks. Peter gave an internal sigh. He envied his brother and his relationship with his wife. Kate was amazing and the perfect fit for Drew. Peter's desire for a wife of his own kept growing every time he saw the two of them together.

And then there was Fiona Gilliam. Peter's eyes sought her out as they always seemed to when she was near. She was off to the side, working by herself to haul a roll of old carpet outside. "Fee! Wait up. Let me help you."

Peter hurried over. His heart gave a little flip at the grin she gave him. "Thanks, but I've got it. This place is going to be so great once you're done." Fiona stood with her hands on her hips, stretching her back.

Peter's eyes quickly took her in. Even standing there covered in dirt and debris, she was stunning. She had tucked her curly red hair underneath a bandana. A few stray wisps had escaped to tickle her forehead. Peter's hands itched to reach out to tuck them back. He clenched his hands to fists to resist the urge to touch her.

"I think you have a higher opinion of this place than I do. It will be livable at least." Peter grinned at her. He could stand here all day talking with her.

"Have some faith, Peter. We're going to make this place awesome." The light reflecting from her mossy green eyes almost took his breath away.

Faith. His grin faded slightly as he thought about how shaky his faith was these days, but Peter certainly couldn't voice that. He was the pastor at Seaside Chapel. How could a pastor not have solid faith? He'd been fighting what felt like an uphill battle ever since he'd arrived in Haven to take over the church. And he was getting tired.

Peter thought it would be easier now that he'd been here a few years. But the congregation had loved Pastor Dan, who had led the church for decades. Peter had no doubt the man would still be here leading his flock if he hadn't died one Sunday morning mid-sermon of a massive heart attack. Even now, five years later, the congregation still spoke about it in hushed whispers.

To say Peter had large shoes to fill when he'd arrived fresh-faced and newly graduated from seminary would be an understatement. He'd been fighting to be accepted by many of the older congregants ever since. It didn't help that Agnes Johnson still didn't think he could run the church without her opinion. She constantly stopped by to talk about everything from the music selections to how the Sunday School should be run. She had an "extra grace required" personality, and he felt like he was running low on grace lately.

Peter ran a hand through his hair. "Either way, it will be nice to get out of the parsonage. I'm pretty sure Drew's spent more time fixing things there than on his own jobs. The place was too big for me, too. I certainly didn't need five bedrooms and three bathrooms. Still, not all the members agreed with my decision to move out to my own place."

Again, understatement. Mrs. Johnson had led the charge on that one. Thankfully Drew had been at the meeting where it was discussed. He had told them how much work was needed to fix the old parsonage. Drew had convinced them it would be more economical to tear it down and create a public space instead. They had finally all, well mostly all, agreed it made more sense to allow a housing allowance for Peter to live elsewhere while they figured out what to do with the old home.

The small bungalow he'd purchased just a few weeks ago was the perfect size for him. The drive would allow him to feel more of a separation from his home life and his work life. Not all pastors wanted that, he knew, but it was something he'd begun to crave more and more over the last few months.

Maybe he just needed a vacation. He couldn't remember the last time he'd taken time for himself since he'd moved here. It was longer than he cared to remember.

Both of his brothers and their significant others had pitched in, as well as Fiona, to help him get the outside of his new place winter tight. They'd just managed it after Drew and Kate returned from their honeymoon. It was now almost Thanksgiving and getting colder. Peter was hoping to have the inside move-in ready before Christmas. It would be a tight deadline, but with his brothers help, he could manage it. He was eager to move out of the old, drafty parsonage.

"Hey, you okay?" Fiona reached out a hand and placed it on his arm. Peter's heart leapt at her touch, but he took a quick step back, out of reach. It wasn't that he didn't want Fee's touch, quite the contrary, he often found himself craving it. And that was becoming the issue.

"Yeah. I'm good. Sorry. Let's get this outside." Peter reached down and lifted one end of the carpet roll and waited for Fiona to grab the other side. He knew he didn't deserve this fantastic woman. He wasn't worthy of Fiona. He was beginning to believe he wasn't worthy of anything.

Chapter 2

♥

F iona worked to hide the slow burn of her anger bubbling below the surface at Peter's rejection of her touch. He had been doing it more often lately, and she was just about ready to smack him. She focused instead on helping the infuriating man wrestle the carpet out to the dumpster.

It didn't make sense. Just mere weeks ago, he had held her in his arms as they had learned the dance moves for Kate and Drew's wedding. She thought something had started to shift in their relationship, but here she was still waiting for Peter to make a move. She wasn't sure how much longer she could wait.

She knew she could be a lot to deal with at times. She could be loud. She had high standards. She liked pretty things. And on top of that, she had a temper and a stubbornness that sometimes got her into trouble. Still, she thought they had started something during those nights of dance lessons leading up to the wedding.

And yet, he'd just stepped back from her casual touch on his arm like she'd burned him. Had she read too much into those lessons? She'd loved how he'd held her so close. She never felt so safe as she had when in Peter's arms. Okay, so he had to hold her that way to dance, but still.

And she was sure he had almost kissed her once. Just the thought of that moment could make her heart skip a beat. She so wanted to know what his lips would feel like on hers. She'd even started to dream about it. There had to be something sacrilegious about dreaming of kissing your pastor.

She didn't think she was a bad judge of character, her past notwithstanding. Her relationship with Hank had thrown her off for a while, but she'd thought she had her groove back. She snorted quietly. Right. She may come across like she had it all together, but mostly she just faked it.

Fiona dusted her hands off on her jeans as Peter hurry back into the house without a word. It was almost like she had some sort of contagious disease. She bit back the growl trying to come out. She needed a minute to calm down or she might just walk back in there and smack some sense into the man, pastor or not!

She began to pace along the side of the dumpster that hid her from the house. She needed to start looking at this whole thing objectively, use her head and not just her heart.

Because her heart was fully involved at this point.

She closed her eyes, tipping her head back and spoke aloud, "God, I know I'm still learning, but I could use a little help. What should I do?"

"Help with what?"

Fiona gave a start as her eyes popped open. Kate was standing in front of her. Fee had been so engrossed in her own thoughts she hadn't heard her best friend's approach. Good thing it had been Kate and not Peter returning. She felt her face warm at the thought.

She held back another snort. Yeah, right. She doubted he was thinking about her now, other than figuring out how to avoid her. "I didn't hear you."

"Obviously. What do you need help with?"

Fiona had been trying to deal with the issue by herself, but maybe it was time to ask her friend for some advice. After all, Kate had just married a Grant brother. She must have some insider information she could share that might help Fiona figure out what made Peter tick.

"Not here." Fiona didn't want to risk Peter sneaking up on her as she laid out her heart.

"I was heading into town to get some things Drew needs. Come with me." Kate looped her arm through Fiona's and tugged her along.

Fiona hesitated for only a moment before she moved to keep up with Kate. "So, relegated to gopher again?" Fiona shot a grin at her friend.

"That man. He thinks I'm helpless, I swear. No matter how often I remind him I did all the work at the store to get it ready. I wasn't doing any rewiring, but still I hung sheetrock, mudded and taped, and I even put up all the shelves for storage."

Fee knew Kate had been having this same argument with Drew since they'd started helping Peter renovate his home. It seemed like Drew thought they were both helpless females who couldn't do anything other than light grunt work and paint. He was constantly finding them jobs with as little labor as possible or running errands.

Secretly, Fiona was sure it wasn't that he didn't trust them. He just might be something of a perfectionist and wanted things done his way.

"Let's grab something from the Three Cats Café for later. Maybe we can use their stomachs to appeal to them." Kate gave Fiona a grin. "I'm not above bribery."

Fiona let out a laugh. She was still thankful she had run into Kate a few years ago outside her store. The poor woman had upended her purse all over the sidewalk looking for her keys. Fiona had been walking by and stopped to help, invited herself in, and never left.

The two women climbed into Drew's truck and drove towards the town of Haven. It wasn't a large town, but it had its own grocery store, hardware store, a few churches other than Seaside Chapel, an elementary school, and a library.

Haven was more of a tourist destination, but there were people who lived there year-round. The town's biggest draw was the long boardwalk which ran parallel to the beach. Kate's small shop, Seascapes, was located on the boardwalk along with a few art galleries, a bookstore, and a few small restaurants.

All the locals, however, always went to the Three Cats Café, which was run by three sisters. It was the place to go on a Friday night after the little league games or on a Saturday morning for pastries. People hung out there to catch up with each other. Living in a small town had its advantages as well as its disadvantages. Everyone always seemed to know what was going on with everyone else. And the café was the hub of all the town gossip.

Usually, Fiona loved that kind of thing, but she didn't want everyone gossiping about her and Peter. She knew she could trust Kate to keep it quiet. She might not even say anything to Drew if Fiona asked nicely.

Kate grinned at her as she drove down the road towards town. "So, are you going to spill it or what? I can see your brain working on it over there. I can practically smell the steam coming out of your ears. Talk."

"What would be your best piece of advice for winning the heart of a Grant man?" Fiona looked out the window, watching through the trees as she spotted glimpses of the coastline. The road Drew and Peter lived on meandered along the shoreline towards Haven.

"Be yourself."

Fiona looked at Kate. "That's it? Be myself." She huffed out a puff of air and felt wisps of hair bouncing on her forehead. "That's what I've been doing, and it hasn't been working. I'm still waiting for the man to make a move."

"Fee, he likes you."

She couldn't help it. She snorted loudly. "Ha! You say that because you're my best friend. That man doesn't know what he likes. And if he likes me, he sure has a funny way of showing it. He practically ran back into the house after helping me move some carpet just before we left. He finds excuses to not be around me. He jumps like a scalded cat if I even seem to breathe wrong around him."

The words were pouring out so fast she placed a hand over her mouth to stop the torrent. She paused for a minute, taking deep breaths, focusing on what Kate had said. She lowered her hand, "Why do you say that?"

"Fee, anyone with eyes can see the man likes you. He watches you constantly, especially if you're busy doing something else. He watches you so much on Sunday that I've seen him lose his place in his sermon. It's actually kind of comical. Drew and I..."

"What? Drew knows? I suppose Lucas and Bree do, too. Anyone else?" Fiona groaned. This was just what she'd wanted to avoid.

"Sweetie, I'm pretty sure the whole town knows. Well, anyone who comes to Seaside on Sunday must suspect something. I'm not sure how they couldn't. The man is besotted with you."

"Besotted? Really? Been reading regency romances again?"

Kate laughed. "Maybe, but it seemed to fit. The two of you are still dancing around each other. One of you is going to have to make a move."

"Well, I was hoping you could tell me what that might be. Because right now, I feel like I have two left feet and don't know the steps."

Fiona let her head fall back against the seat as her mind whirled. If she believed what Kate was telling her, Peter did like her as more than a friend. And there was no reason why she shouldn't believe her. Kate wouldn't lie to her.

Fiona squared her shoulders and sat up straight. "What's your best piece of advice? Because I'm not sure how much longer I can stand this whole not dancing thing. I really like dancing with Peter." A soft sigh escaped as she slumped back against the seat.

Kate pulled into a parking space in front of the café before replying. "Fee, we just need to figure out how to get Peter to get out of his own head and make a move. I think he's so focused on others he sometimes forgets he's allowed to have a life."

"What do you mean?"

"I know he's had a rough time taking over the church. There are still a lot of folks there who miss Pastor Dan."

"Wait, seriously? How long has Peter been here? It's been a few years, hasn't it? And it's not like Pastor Dan is coming back." Fiona gave a rueful wince. She wasn't trying to be disrespectful, but seriously, it wasn't like the man had just quit and left. He was dead after all.

"Yeah, but you forget," Kate continued, "Peter has people like Mrs. Johnson in his life."

"Right. Mrs. Johnson. What's her issue do you think?"

"No clue. But she isn't happy with anything Peter has done at the church since he took over. She makes it hard for him."

"It seems to be her superpower." Fiona gave Kate a wry grin. They'd all had run-ins with Mrs. Johnson over the years. Her hobby seemed to be making everyone's life miserable.

Kate turned on the truck seat to look at Fiona. "I think it might be time for me and Drew to become 'too busy,'" she made air quotes around the words, "to help Peter on his renovation. And I think you need an overdue vacation from the store. It's the slow season anyway. Become indispensable to him. Show him how wonderful you are. Because you really are wonderful, Fee."

"You might want to wait until Drew's finished the wiring. I can do most anything else but messing with electricity scares me."

Kate laughed. "Peter has the skills to do it on his own. He has all the skills he needs. Their father taught all of them what to do. Mr. G wanted to make sure all his kids, foster and biological, could do anything they needed to fix a house or a car or pretty much anything else."

"Okay, then. Let's get whatever Drew needs and get back. Operation Catch a Pastor is in motion." Fiona laughed along with Kate before taking a deep breath.

Show Peter he needed her. She gave a resolved nod. Yeah, she could do that. A grin spread over her face. She just might enjoy this project after all.

Chapter 3

♥

P eter had begged out of a planning meeting for the holiday schedule at the church to work on his house tonight. He knew he shouldn't, but he wasn't really needed, and he knew it. The women's auxiliary would do what they usually did, and he would be there just for show. He didn't like wasting time in useless meetings.

He knew the church should come first. It needed to be his top priority. However, he was motivated to get his house to a point where he could move in. He couldn't stand the thought of many more nights in the old parsonage where the wind came seeping in around the windows, rippling the old curtains, and overwhelming the heat registers. It felt like it was almost breathing, and it gave him the creeps. Not that he would ever admit it to anyone.

He was a little annoyed as well. He tried to push it away as he worked on running the wiring to the new bathroom light he'd installed earlier. Drew had given him an excuse as to why he couldn't come help tonight. Something lame. Just like he had for the last two nights. The work was slowing with no extra hands to help.

When Peter had tried Lucas next, he'd been out on a date with Bree. Peter didn't want to beg for the help. Besides, there really was nothing he couldn't do on his own. He wanted the help to make it go faster. And wasn't that what brothers were for? To help when you needed it. He pushed out a breath of frustration as he continued to follow the line from the junction box back to the switch.

Yeah, he couldn't blame either of his brothers, even though he wanted to. Peter worked to push the annoyance away. He knew Drew wanted to spend time with Kate and Lucas wanted to be with Bree, especially now that they were engaged to be married. Peter was the odd man out.

He gave a sigh as he kept working. If he could get the wiring done tonight, he'd be able to start putting up drywall this weekend. Peter decided he wouldn't ask for help anymore. Nope. His brothers knew his deadline was to spend Christmas in this house. If they helped, great. If not, well, then Peter would be spending a few more cold winter nights in the parsonage. He would just have to live with it.

A knock at the door brought a smile to his face. It seemed one of his brothers had a change of heart. His grin spread as he moved to the living room. "You don't have to knock, you know!"

Peter yanked open the door, ready to give whichever brother was there a hard time. The words died in his throat and his brain immediately turned off. Fiona was standing on his doorstep, pizza box held in one hand and a paper bag in the other.

Her hair was covered by a grey beanie with her long hair flowing down her back. She had on a parka with a fur collar, turned up around her neck and matching grey mittens. Her jeans were tucked into a pair of boots which ended just below her knees. Peter tried to find his voice, but his mouth had gone dry at the sight of her.

"Hungry?" She lifted the bag as she moved from foot to foot to stay warm. The wind was starting to pick up making the temperature drop.

"What?" Peter shook himself out of his stupor. Fiona had that power over him.

"Are. You. Hungry?" Fiona said each word, careful to enunciate it fully. "Because I am, and I'm also cold. Let me in." She didn't wait for Peter to respond. She shoved the pizza box in his arms and pushed past him to the kitchen area.

Peter shook himself and shut the door. Not a brother. Fee. He felt his chest tighten as he turned and walked towards the kitchen area. Alone with Fee. A dream and a nightmare all rolled into one.

He wouldn't dwell on the fact he was here alone with her. Nope. He would focus on the fact she was here, and she had brought food. He could play it cool. He *would* play it cool. It wasn't like he couldn't control himself. No, that wasn't the issue. He didn't want to come across as an awkward idiot. The odds were not in his favor.

Peter had set up an impromptu table to use when working on the house. It was just a slab of plywood propped on top of two sawhorses. Four upturned buckets sat around it from the last shared meal.

Fiona pushed aside a roll of 14 gauge wire and set the bag down on the table before taking off her coat and mittens.

"Brrr...the temperature is dropping fast." She rubbed her hands together over the pellet stove in the corner pumping out heat before busying herself unpacking plates and plasticware from the bag. "Go wash your hands and we can eat. Hurry up, I'm starving!"

She tossed a brilliant smile at him, and Peter felt his heart skip a beat or two. He gulped. He walked like a robot to the kitchen sink, which he had finally finished hooking up last week, and washed his hands. He took an extra second to dry them. *Hold it together, man. It's not like you haven't talked to a pretty girl before.* Yeah, right. This was Fiona, who was he kidding?

Turning back to Fiona, he asked "What are you doing here?"

"I'm here to help. I figured you hadn't eaten anything, so I brought food. Here I am, saving the day once again." She held out her arms wide and gave him a mega-watt smile.

He felt lightning bolts zip through his body. Her smile could do that to him. He needed to get a grip. He was around women all the time. No one else had this affect over him but Fee. He needed to figure out a way to deal with it and fast.

"Ok." He rubbed a hand through his hair. *Get a grip, Grant.* He was being ridiculous. This was innocent. A friend helping a friend. There was nothing wrong with Fiona being here. They were two adults. He needed to stop worrying about what people like Mrs. Johnson would say if he was seen alone in his home with a single woman, especially one from the congregation.

And he needed to get his brain back on track or who knew what stupid thing he might say in front of this beautiful and vivacious woman. He swallowed hard. That line of thinking wasn't helping.

"Is this okay?" Fiona had stopped and stared at him looking worried.

"Of course." Peter gave his own smile back as he shook off the thoughts. Mrs. Johnson wasn't here. He could make his own decisions. And he *was* hungry after all. "Let's eat. I'm starving. I haven't had anything since lunch, and that was about six hours ago."

Fiona smiled back and finished pulling drinks and napkins from the bag. "I got mushrooms and pepperoni. I know it's your favorite."

"It is! I can't believe you remembered that."

"Well, you like fungus." She gave an exaggerated shudder. "Ugh."

Peter laughed and realized it was genuine. He hadn't done that since... Well, maybe since the last time he had been alone with Fiona practicing dance steps in her apartment. He felt some of the tension ease from his shoulders.

"Let me pray so we can eat." The two sat down on the buckets, knees almost touching.

"Sure." Fiona extended a hand to him, and Peter quickly hid his surprise. Of course. They always held hands when they prayed, but usually he made sure there was a buffer between Fiona and himself, so he wasn't holding her hand. There was no buffer tonight.

He reached out and closed her hand in his and tried desperately not to think about how good her smaller hand felt wrapped inside his. He didn't want to think about how soft her skin was or how warm her hand felt.

Swallowing hard, he began, "Dear Lord," he stopped and cleared his throat, "we thank You for your provision of food for our evening meal tonight. Thank You for the hands which prepared it for our bodies, as well as the hands which delivered it." He couldn't help squeezing Fiona's hand in thanks. His stomach gave a small flip when she squeezed back. "You are our Great God and Provider. Be with us as we work tonight and keep us safe. In Your name I pray, amen."

Peter slid his hand reluctantly away from Fiona's and smiled warmly at her. "I meant that. Thank you for bringing me supper. I usually just keep going until I can't stand the hunger pangs anymore and then go home to figure out what might be edible in my fridge. This will help keep me going tonight."

"My pleasure. What are you working on?" Fiona flipped open the pizza box and took out a slice, cheese holding on until it finally popped free. She put a second slice on another plate and handed it to Peter. She began to pick the mushrooms off her slice, adding them to Peter's.

Peter grinned, bemused. "Thanks." He picked up the slice and took a large bite. Chewing fast, he was hungrier than he realized, he swallowed before continuing. "Wiring. I'd like to get it done so I can get the sheetrock hung on Saturday. That's if I can get my sermon done by Friday." Peter shoved another large bite of pizza in his mouth.

"What's your sermon about this week?"

He held up a finger as he finished the bite he had just taken. "I'm continuing with Hebrews. We're up to chapter 11 so we'll be talking about faith." Peter felt a hitch in his spirit. Faith. The thing he'd been struggling with the most in recent weeks.

"Tell me more."

He had Fiona's full attention. He could feel the weight of her eyes on him. It was a bit heady to have the focus of a beautiful woman on him. What Peter wouldn't give to have Fiona fully in his life as well. To sit like this over pizza or any meal, alone, talking about their day, his sermons, or whatever else they had going on in their lives. He could get used to it.

He knew he shouldn't enjoy this too much. He should put up a barrier, something to hold Fiona at arm's length. He knew he could fall for this woman easily, but he wasn't sure if that was the right decision for him at this point in time. He pushed the thought away as he decided to just enjoy her company. There was no harm in that.

Before he realized it, the rest of the evening had flown by. Peter found himself becoming more and more relaxed as he worked side by side with Fiona. Her ready laugh had him chuckling along with her. He hadn't had this much fun working on his house since the last time Fiona had helped him.

"What time is it?" Fiona yawned loudly and rubbed her back. "I may be in danger of turning into a pumpkin."

Peter glanced at his watch, eyes widening. "It's closing in on midnight! I'm sorry, Fee. I shouldn't have kept you out this late. I should have been in bed hours ago. I have an early morning tomorrow."

"Are you working again tomorrow night? I'm free. I could swing back over with sandwiches from the Three Cats this time if you'd like help." Fiona paused in pulling on her hat to wait for Peter's answer.

Peter paused. His heart and his gut wanted to give a resounding yes, but his head was telling him to be careful. He pushed the thoughts away though. He'd had a great time with Fiona tonight, and he wanted to see her again. This was nothing more than a friend helping a friend. And he'd tell Mrs. Johnson as much if she said anything. Because if Mrs. Johnson ever knew Fiona was here this late, she *would* say something.

Swallowing hard, he decided to do what he wanted for a change. "Yeah. That would be great, but I'll grab the sandwiches on my way here. What time do you get done at the store? We can eat and then finish up this. Your help means I'll be able to hang drywall Saturday after all."

"Kate gave me some time off from the store." Fiona shrugged. "I'm free all day if you want to start earlier."

Peter eyed Fiona. "Vacation in November? Are you planning to visit your family for Thanksgiving?" He'd been hoping to sit across from her at Kate's table. His stomach twisted slightly at the thought of not seeing Fiona for a few days.

"No, I'll be here. I had a bunch of time off built up. I decided to take a couple weeks off before the holiday rush. Kate can handle the store with the part-time help we have." Fiona waved her hand in the air, dismissing any other concerns, "So, what time should I swing by?"

Peter's brain was working frantically on his schedule. If he moved the elders meeting, again, he could be here by two at the latest. It would give him even more time with Fiona.

"I'll text you. I need to check my schedule at the office tomorrow first." Not a lie. He knew his schedule, but something was holding him back from saying yes immediately. He didn't want to appear over eager to be with her. He didn't know why, but something just told him to go slow, as if he hadn't been doing just that for the last few weeks.

Peter flipped on the outside light and opened the door just as a large vehicle slowed at the end of his driveway. He wondered vaguely who it might be. A small town meant just about everyone knew he was here working on his new place. Maybe it was someone looking for him? He shook off the thought. Not at midnight. It was likely just someone slowing down for an animal in the road.

"What is it?" Fiona reached out a hand to steady herself on his arm as she turned on the steps to look where Peter was staring.

Horror slowly began to sink into Peter's thoughts as he recognized the car. There was only one person in Haven who drove a robin's egg blue Hummer.

"Oh no," Fiona breathed just as the brake lights faded around the corner. "She's not going to like this is she?"

"Not even a little." Peter would be dealing with Mrs. Johnson once more tomorrow, bright and early. He had no doubt about it.

Chapter 4

♥

M om, I'm on my way. It will take me about four hours to get there depending on what the roads are like once I hit Island Falls. You know how they get the further north you go." Fiona tossed a few extra pairs of socks in her suitcase. Her grandmother's house, located in northern Maine, could be cold this time of year.

They had been trying for years to get Grandma Josie to move south, closer to family, but she refused to leave the farmhouse her grandfather had built back in the late 1800s. Potato country. God's country. It was all the same to Grandma. Her ancestors had harvested truckloads of potatoes over the years from their small family farm.

Fiona remembered the year her mother had sent her up in early September for the potato harvest. She'd thought it would be fun. She'd been wrong. Children started school weeks earlier than those down south so that they could take time off for the harvest. They swarmed the fields pulling potatoes as fast as they could, tossing them into buckets, then dumping the full buckets into larger barrels. Fiona had been about thirteen. She had lasted a day before tapping out.

Other farms used more modern methods, but Grandma Josie still liked to do it old school. No tractors for her come harvest time. Nope. All those fields of potatoes were hand harvested. It was back breaking work and mostly done by young teens.

Aroostook County, the top of Maine, where the only things that seemed to grow were moose, potatoes, and the snowbanks. Kids up in 'The County', as everyone called it, were tougher than Fiona, and she hadn't cared. She'd come home that first night covered head to toe in dirt, sweat, and even a few tears. She'd taken a long shower and refused to go anywhere near the fields the next day.

Grandma Josie wouldn't hear of it though. She let Fee off from picking, but she spent the next few days sorting spuds. Fiona wasn't sure which had been harder, but she'd never been so happy to leave the farm that year. She always made sure she had other plans during harvest time after that. She never visited Grandma Josie in September again.

But now, her grandmother needed her. Grandma Josie had taken a tumble on the ice. Thankfully nothing was broken, but she was banged up and bruised. It must be bad if Fiona's mother was asking her to go check on her grandma. Of course, Grandma Josie hadn't asked for help. She was too ornery and independent for that. She hated it when people, as she said, fussed over her.

Susan, Fiona's cousin, had called to tell them about the fall. Susan was days away from delivering her third child and had her hands full. No one else lived close enough to deal with Grandma Josie.

"As soon as I'm done packing, I'll head out. I should make it to Bangor before dark at least." Fiona closed her suitcase and gave one final look around. She would call Kate from the road. And Peter... Well, she wasn't sure what was going on there. She hadn't heard from the infernal man since Mrs. Johnson had done a drive by at midnight and seen her leaving his house two days ago.

He hadn't texted her to let her know what time to show up the next day to help him. All the texts she had sent remained unanswered. He had ghosted her. No texts. No calls. Radio silence.

And now she was leaving to head north before Sunday morning. She had plans to confront him at church where he couldn't avoid her.

She'd heard through the church grapevine Mrs. Johnson had shown up bright and early the next day and dressed Peter down. *He* hadn't told her this. Nope. She'd heard it from Kate who had heard it from someone else, likely Drew.

Fiona had asked Kate, "Why on earth was the old biddy out that way anyway?"

"She told Peter she'd been out visiting someone down the road and lost track of time."

Fiona snorted at the memory. That seemed like a lie if ever she heard one, but really, how would she really know. She knew nothing about Mrs. Johnson's social life. Thank goodness.

Her mother's voice brought her back and she looked to see what else she needed. "Be careful. The roads might be a little slick."

Tucking her phone between her ear and her shoulder, she went to grab her toiletries from the bathroom. "I know, Mom. I'll call you when I get there. She does know I'm coming, right?"

Fiona's red hair and temper came from Grandma Josie's side of the family. She didn't want to show up unannounced on her grandmother's doorstep. Especially if her grandmother thought Fiona was being sent to check on her.

"I thought it best if someone just went. I would have asked your brother, but he's working on his thesis, and it's due just after the holidays. You'd mentioned taking some time off work, so I thought you might be able to head up."

"So, Grandma Josie doesn't know I'm coming. Wonderful." Fiona didn't bother to hide the sarcasm.

She'd taken the time off to spend with Peter, to show him how much he needed her, not to babysit her grandmother. Now she was going to leave without having gotten much further than showing him how good she was at handing him the tool he needed. Operation Catch a Pastor was not going as planned.

"She's pushing eighty years old, Fee. She needs some help even if she doesn't think she does. Just go and make sure she's eating right and not doing too much."

Fiona held back the snort trying to come out. "You owe me."

Fiona's mother laughed. "It'll be fine, sweetie. Her bark is worse than her bite. Susan said there was some bruising on her face and the hospital was concerned about a concussion. She's going to stay with grandma until you get there. Mom twisted her ankle too and was limping around. Just make sure she's doing okay. I'll make you a batch of cookies next time you visit."

"Frosted molasses cookies *and* whoopie pies. Like I said, you owe me."

"Deal. Drive safe."

Fiona hung up and grabbed her keys. It was going to be a long drive to Presque Isle, and she wanted to make as much of it as she could before it got too dark.

After she hauled her luggage out to the car, she ran back inside to make one last check. Snatching up her phone where she'd left it on the counter, she stopped to breathe. She wasn't going to let Peter get away with ignoring her. She hated when people did that.

She swiped open her phone to send him another text message. *Hey, just wanted to let you know I'm heading north. My grandma fell and needs help for a little bit. Not sure how long I'll be gone. Hoping we can do sandwiches when I'm back.*

Fiona read it over. It wasn't too pushy and said the basics. Maybe this was for the best. Maybe this would help him realize he would miss her. Wouldn't that be amazing?

She gave a start as her phone dinged for an incoming text. *Sorry to hear that. I'll be praying.*

Fiona stared at the screen. He'd ignored all other texts over the last few days but responded to this one. She wasn't sure if she should be happy or angry he'd responded at all. She was still glaring at the screen as a second message popped up. *Drive safe*.

A smile curved her lips. That was the equivalent of an "I love you." Everyone knew that to be true. Peter might not know it yet, but he was on his way for falling for her. She just needed to tweak the plan.

Chapter 5

♥

N o, dear, not like that. Here, let me do it. It'll be faster."

Fiona wondered if she could convince a jury it had been a mercy killing. Anyone who spent time in the kitchen with her grandmother would understand, she was sure.

She gritted her teeth and began counting to ten before pausing. Her grandmother had been trying to teach her how to cook almost since she'd arrived. Fiona was getting better but sharing her grandmother's kitchen required patience she often didn't have.

She stood back and watched as Grandma Josie picked up the bowl under one arm and took the wooden spoon in the other. She began whipping the batter with nothing less than brute strength, beating it into submission.

Fiona knew how to make a cake. Why they needed one, she had no idea, but her grandmother was insisting. And apparently, she didn't think Fiona could beat it correctly. Grandma also didn't believe in having an electric mixer or any other "newfangled" appliance which might make life easier. She didn't even own a microwave.

It had been four long weeks since Fiona had arrived at her grandmother's farm in Presque Isle. She'd been here two weeks longer than she wanted, and it looked like she wasn't leaving anytime soon. It didn't matter that she had a job down south. Nope. It seemed everyone and the weather was conspiring against her.

By the look of her, no one would ever know Grandma Josie had had a mild concussion, a sprained ankle, and bruises from her fall on the ice just before Thanksgiving. She'd recovered well for a woman almost in her eighties. Yet, every time Fiona went to leave, the old woman dropped subtle hints at her, creating gut churning guilt at the thought of driving away.

"Sure would be nice to have family here for the holidays this year" or "I've enjoyed having you around, but I understand if you have to get back. I'll be okay here all alone." Grandma Josie was the queen of subtle guilt trips. She would, if confronted, deny it, but Fiona still felt the effect.

Now they were closing in on Christmas, and there had been one snowstorm after the other since Fiona had arrived. Sure, there had been times when she'd thought she'd be able to escape back to the coast, but then Grandma Josie would toss out another zinger. "You remind me a lot of myself when I was your age. It's been nice having some young blood around here, but you have a life to get back to, I understand."

So, here Fiona stood in the kitchen watching her grandmother make a cake for Christmas morning two days away. "We need to celebrate His birthday, honey. I used to always do this when your mom was little. Didn't she continue this tradition with you and your brother?"

Fiona had been surprised to learn her grandmother was such a strong Christian. Fiona's mother had never done anything when they were small to make Fiona think she had been raised in such a faith-filled household. "No, Gram, Mom never baked a cake on Christmas."

When Fiona had spent vacations here, she went to church with Grandma Josie but never really made the connection that her grandmother lived out what was said from the pulpit each week. Intermittent visits weren't enough to really get to know what her grandmother believed.

Grandma Josie attended a nice little congregation not far from where she lived. Fiona was the youngest there by more than twenty years, but the pastor had been friendly and, more importantly, theologically correct as far as Fiona could determine. She was still trying to figure out what had happened to make her mother turn her back on it all. Christ had not been part of Fiona's life until she met Peter.

Peter. She missed him something dreadful and more than once, just the thought of seeing him again, had pulled her to her car. One day she'd even started it and sat there, thinking of her lonely grandmother in her big house all by herself for the holidays. Fiona had turned it off and gone inside before she changed her mind.

The only good thing about being gone were the texts. Peter had continued sending her quick responses to her messages. Nothing too life changing, but he was communicating with her. And she could work with that, had been working with that, for the last few weeks.

She pulled her phone out of her back pocket and thumbed it open, pulling up the last text from Peter.

I'm feeling a little stressed. Can you pray for me?

She scrolled back to read a few others, needing the reminder that he thought of her from time to time.

Wow! That snowbank is massive! This Florida native is awed!

Fiona had sent a photo she'd taken in the middle of the driveway. She'd stuck her phone in the snowbank across from her. Then, standing on tiptoes, she'd spread her arms as far as she could reach overhead, but they'd still fallen a few inches short of the top.

Come visit me. I miss you.

That was the last text she'd sent two days prior. She'd received nothing back until the prayer request he'd sent this morning. Nothing to acknowledge her request to see him. She knew it would be a gamble, but the words had just fallen onto the keyboard and her fingertip had tapped send before she could rethink it.

"Grandma, I'll stay until Christmas, but I need to head home after that. There's something I need to deal with. I've been gone long enough as it is."

Fiona didn't want her grandmother to know she had someone special. She wasn't sure she was ready to have *that* discussion with her grandmother. Besides, she didn't even know if she *did* have someone special.

"What's his name?"

Fiona's head whipped up as she watched her grandmother place the bowl on the counter. She had to give her grandmother credit. She didn't even bother trying to deflect the conversation.

"Peter."

Grandma Josie had a twinkle in her eye as she looked at Fiona. "You afraid he won't be there when you get back? Any man worth his salt will still be there waiting for you. He give you a promise yet?"

"Not yet. And he'll still be there. I just don't want him to have time to think he can live without me around."

Fiona felt her face blushing as the words slipped out of her mouth, but it was the truth. Anyone could come along and snag him away from her while she was getting frostbite up here.

"Well, it seems you might need to head home after all. Help me with this cake and tell me more about your man."

Fiona smiled. She liked the sound of that.

"He's the brother of my best friend's husband."

"Say that again, sweetie? That's a lot of whos-its and whats-its."

Fiona laughed. Yes, while her grandmother did drive her bonkers some days, there had been more good days than bad. Fiona had enjoyed getting to know Grandma Josie better.

"Kate Grant is my best friend. She owns the shop I work at."

"That's right. But what does she have to do with your beau?"

"He's not my beau. Kate is married to Drew Grant and Peter is Drew's brother."

"Ahhh, well that makes sense now. Tell me more about this Peter."

"He's the pastor of the church I go to, Seaside Chapel."

"What kind of name is that for a church?"

Fiona stared at her grandmother. "What do you mean? What's wrong with it?"

"Chapel? Is it tiny? Why isn't it called Seaside Baptist Church? Are they too afraid to say what denomination it is? It's not one of those newfangled ones, is it? Not sure I could handle going to a church that didn't have a proper name."

Her grandmother continued moving about the kitchen, giving orders. "Grab that pan and give it a good wipe with some shortening, honey. Use the paper towel in the container."

Fiona did as her grandmother commanded, continuing with the conversation. "Seaside Chapel isn't small. It's a regular size church, about the size of your church actually."

"Hummph. Still seems like a weird name to me, but whatever floats your boat. What does he look like?"

Fiona hid a smile as she put the Crisco away and brought the pan to her grandmother. "He's about three or four inches taller than me, not too much. I can just tip my head back to look him in the eyes without looking up his nose." She smiled and shrugged her shoulders as her grandmother laughed.

"And when have you stood face to face with your pastor, young lady, to notice something like that?"

Fiona did laugh now, not trying to hide it. "At Kate and Drew's wedding a couple months ago. We were paired up because I was the maid of honor, and he was the best man. We had to dance together."

"And how was that?"

"Fabulous." Fiona barely held back the sigh that wanted to come out at the thought of what it had felt like in Peter's arms.

"Well, let's pray this storm lets up soon and you can head home to this fabulous man of yours."

Grandma Josie slid the Christmas cake into the oven. Pray. Maybe Fiona had been praying for the wrong thing after all.

Chapter 6

♥

P eter lifted his head at the knock. His brother, Lucas, stood there with a light covering of snow on his shoulders and a dusting in his hair. "Got a second?"

Peter smiled at his brother. "Sure. For you, anytime."

Lucas slowly crossed to the front of Peter's desk. He took his jacket off, tossing it on the coach, and brushed a hand through his wet hair before sitting.

"Is this a friendly visit with your brother or something more serious with your pastor?"

"Maybe both." Lucas gave him a grin.

"I'm listening." Peter leaned back in his chair and waited. Lucas always thought things through. And Peter had worked on his listening skills since taking over Seaside Chapel. At first, he'd found it hard to sit and be quiet, but now he'd learned to enjoy it over the years.

"Bree and I want to get married."

Peter held back the laughter trying to spill out. His brother hadn't smiled at the statement. Peter kept the grin on his face. Lucas and Bree were engaged after all.

When Lucas didn't continue, Peter prompted him, "And?"

"We don't want to wait for the spring. We want to do it soon."

"I'm confused. What's changed?" Peter eyed his brother with a raised eyebrow.

"Nothing. Nothing's changed. Peter, c'mon, you know me better than that. We just decided we didn't want to wait any longer. This whole dating and engaged thing is getting harder to do." Lucas cleared his throat and sat back.

Peter watched with amusement as a tinge of red crawled up his brother's neck. Peter did trust his brother, but he still felt, as his pastor, that he needed to be sure he knew what was going on. "Care to elaborate?"

"I want to be Bree's husband and not her boyfriend. How's that for an answer?" Lucas sat all the way back and crossed his arms. "I'm done waiting and so is she. When's the soonest you can perform the ceremony?"

Peter couldn't hold back his laughter any longer. "Let me check. Are you planning on telling anyone?"

"We thought we'd do a quick ceremony, minimal witnesses. Likely just you, Fiona, Drew, and Kate, maybe a few others."

Peter's breath caught at how casually his brother lumped him in with Fiona. He carefully let out his breath as he pulled up his calendar on his computer.

Lucas hadn't realized how his words affected Peter. He continued explaining, "We'd still do the big wedding thing in the spring as planned. We're not going to hide the fact we're married now. Bree thought everyone would still want to see the ceremony, even if we're already married. We're just done waiting."

"I could do it next weekend if you wanted, after the holiday. Or did you want to do it after the Christmas Eve service? It will make for a late night, but I think we could pull it off. Otherwise, next weekend might be better. New Year's maybe?"

"If you can do Christmas Eve, let's go for it. We aren't going to be elaborate, just done and legal." Lucas cleared his throat, "And this is going to sound nuts, but Bree wants to do it at the café."

"How quiet do you think that'll be?"

"I know, but it's sort of where we met for the first time. The sisters have agreed to it already. Let me just double check they're okay with us being there on Christmas Eve starting at...when?"

"The service here ends by seven. Let's plan for an hour to regroup. We'll meet there at eight o'clock but start about thirty minutes later. Good?"

"Yeah, I'll talk to the sisters and Bree and confirm with you later today."

"I'm happy for you, man. If you head over to the town hall now, you should have your marriage license in time. You know, to make it all legal and done." Peter shot a bemused grin at his brother.

Lucas popped up. "Right. License. What else do I need?"

Peter enjoyed seeing Lucas nervous. He was typically all confident given his police training. He never seemed to let anything trip him up. It was good to see Bree had that effect on him, which made Peter think of Fee.

Swallowing his emotions away, he answered Lucas. "That's it. I'll see you at the Three Cats at eight o'clock on Christmas Eve. Congrats, brother." Peter stood and gave his brother a hug before Lucas hurried out, intent on his errand to become married in about forty-eight hours.

Peter dropped back into his chair. Now both of his brothers would be married. He was starting to feel more and more left out. And it didn't help that the woman who had him tied in knots was still four hours away.

He pulled out his phone to look at the last text she'd sent. *Did you know you can make cake from potatoes?? It's yummy. I'll make it for you sometime.*

He smiled at the words. Potato cake did not sound yummy, but if Fiona made it for him, he would eat it. He'd enjoyed texting with Fiona over the last few weeks. It seemed safer to put his thoughts into writing rather than speech. He felt like he could be himself without stumbling over what he wanted to say. Yet, he still found himself holding back.

After all, he was only supposed to be friends with Fiona. He just couldn't figure out how to manage it – even when she wasn't anywhere in sight.

He tapped on the screen to open the keyboard and typed a text to Fiona before he could overthink it. *Lucas and Bree are going to get married Christmas Eve. Can you come home?*

Home. It almost felt like Peter was asking Fiona into his house, into his life. His phone dinged almost immediately, pulling him away from the thought of what it would be like to have Fiona as his wife.

WHAT!! What happened to the May date?

Nothing. They just want to be married sooner rather than later. Still doing the ceremony in May.

Ok. Let me see what I can do. If the snowstorms give me a window of opportunity, I'll be there.

I'll be praying for the weather to cooperate.

And Peter would. He missed having Fiona pop over to his house with pizza or into the office with a cup of coffee. He missed Fiona's presence in his life. He flopped back into his chair. He missed her smile and her laugh. He missed having her in his life.

He was in trouble. He didn't normally miss friends the way he missed Fiona. He groaned and put his head back on the chair. He was losing the battle of being single. Maybe it was time to rethink things.

"Young man, we need to talk."

Peter's head snapped up as Mrs. Johnson marched into his office. He really needed to find someone to help at the church, an assistant. If for no other reason than to save him from Agnes Johnson bursting in on him like this. If he hadn't been so consumed with thoughts of Fiona, he would have heard her monstrous Hummer pull in.

"What can I do for you, Mrs. Johnson? I don't have long. I have an appointment in twenty minutes."

Peter thought about the twist of words. He *was* meeting Drew at the café, but it was only to help Peter figure out if he'd missed anything on his renovations. He was almost done and couldn't wait to move in. All the same, he shifted uncomfortably.

"Fine. I can cover what I need to say in five." Mrs. Johnson settled herself in the chair in front of his desk, not even taking off her coat.

Peter settled back into his chair and waited for the woman to begin.

"Your attentions are divided." Mrs. Johnson stated this with a stiff nod of her head, punctuating the words.

Peter sat up. "My attentions are what?

"Divided. Anyone can see it."

"Mrs. Johnson, I'm not following you. My attentions are fully devoted to Seaside Chapel and my role here. My personal life has little bearing on what I do at the church." *And it's not like I have a huge personal life anyway,* Peter thought.

Mrs. Johnson continued to steamroll her way forward, "Your focus as head pastor needs to be on Seaside Chapel and the people who attend. Were you aware Cheryl McKenna was in the hospital? Have you been to see her? And poor Charles Philbrick is also a patient at County General. He's had a minor heart attack."

"When did this all happen? I was just there yesterday visiting. I don't remember seeing them there."

Mrs. Johnson fiddled with her purse strap. A sign, Peter knew meant she wasn't being as truthful with him as she should be. "They were both admitted this morning, but still. If you were as fully focused on Seaside Chapel, as you should be, you would already know this."

"I am only one man, Mrs. Johnson. I have no secretary or assistant. I can only do so much."

"If you weren't spending so much time renovating that home you plan to move into, you would have known all of this."

And there it was.

"I don't see how that plays a role. I'm always available by phone. Everyone knows how to reach me. Now, I need to leave for my appointment." Peter stood, picking up his phone. "Was there anything else?"

"Yes. Have you thought more about the conversation we had a few weeks ago about your, well, your clandestine activities?"

Peter tried but couldn't stop a bark of laughter. "My what?"

Mrs. Johnson scowled. "You know exactly what I'm talking about, young man! Don't pretend otherwise."

"I thought I made it clear my 'clandestine activities,' as you call them, were innocent. It was a friend helping a friend and nothing more. In addition, it happened over a month ago. You need to let it go."

Mrs. Johnson pulled herself to her feet and faced Peter, all five feet of her, like a bantam rooster. "You mark me, that woman is trouble. All that red hair. Everyone knows how much passion women like that have. If you're not careful, she'll ruin you and your place here at Seaside. Don't say I didn't warn you." With a loud sniff and a head tilt, the old woman marched from the room.

Peter sank back into his chair. How could he ever get past the prejudice the woman brought to Seaside? Mrs. Johnson didn't make idle threats. She would follow through on whatever she thought was best for the church. The church was her sole focus in life it seemed.

He'd started to think about what it would be like to date Fiona. But now? He'd seen Fiona's temper flare. The women's auxiliary wouldn't stand for it, and neither would Agnes Johnson. The confrontations would be epic, and he would be drawn into the middle of them. He was tired of dealing with all the conflict.

"Lord, what do I do now?"

Chapter 7

♥

G ram, have you seen my eyeliner?" Fiona moved quickly from one place to another, trying to find everything she had strewn about over the last few weeks. She was
throwing things in her bag, praying for the weather to hold.
The news said they would have snowfall by that evening.

While the weather would be perfect for Christmas Eve
and the wedding tonight, Fiona needed to be on the road
in the next ten minutes if she wanted to get back to Haven
in time for the nuptials. While she didn't want to miss the
wedding, she was more eager to finally see Peter in person
after all this time.

She held back the sigh at another Grant wedding. She felt
moisture building in her eyes, but she wasn't going to let it
fall. She couldn't find her waterproof mascara. If she started
crying, she would need to replace what she was wearing once
she was home.

"Here it is, dear."

Fiona turned to take the makeup from her grandmother's
outstretched hand. "Thanks, Gram. I'm sorry I'm running
off like this. I was planning to stay until after Christmas."

"It's okay, dear. Susan will be over to check on me like she usually does, and she'll bring that cute new baby of hers with her. I do like babies."

Stepping forward, Fiona took her grandmother in her arms and pulled her in for a hug. "Move south. Mom would love to have you. Come with me."

Fiona felt rather than heard her grandmother snort before she stepped back. Grandma Josie looked into her eyes, "I highly doubt it, but it's nice of you to say." She patted Fiona's cheek and walked over to the counter to grab the cookies she had packed for Fiona to take.

Taking the cookies, Fiona said, "Mom loves you."

"I know, honey. And I love her too. But it's better that there's a few hundred miles between us."

Fiona hadn't found out what happened between her grandmother and her mother in the time she'd been here. She couldn't imagine what had created a wedge between them.

"What happened, Gram?"

"Nothing you need to worry about, honey. It was just a misunderstanding a long time ago we let fester. We'll fix it one day. Now, let's get you packed up and back home to your man. You need to leave soon if you're going to make that wedding of your friends."

"If you need anything, call me, Gram. I can be here in a few hours."

"Thank you, dear. Now go. Drive safe!"

Fiona gave her grandmother one last kiss and hug before hurrying out the door to her car. The sun was near blinding where it hit the snow and reflected into her eyes. She hadn't wanted to come to Presque Isle, but she didn't regret her time here. She felt she knew Grandma Josie a little bit better.

Grabbing her sunglasses, she slid into her seat and started the car. Waving to where Grandma Josie stood watching, she pulled out and pointed her car south toward home. Home to Peter.

She turned on her radio, switching dials until K-Love came on. Fiona began singing along to the worship music pouring from her speakers. It was a perfect day to drive home and see "her man," as Gram had called him. Her man indeed. Operation Catch a Pastor was back on in full force.

Night was just falling as Fiona pulled into her driveway, her eyes bleary. She turned off her car, just breathing for a minute. The snow had held off. She opened her door and stood. Placing her hands on her hips, she groaned as she stretched. It was a long, boring drive from The County back to the coast. The highway only took her so far, then it was following bumpy state routes after that.

She only had a few hours before she needed to be at the café to help decorate. How Bree had managed to pull together a wedding in just forty-eight hours, she'll never know.

Popping the trunk, Fiona reached in to gather her things. She fumbled the bag of cookies Gram had given her and they fell to the ground.

"Need a hand?"

Fiona whirled, "Peter." She spoke his name in a breath. Before she could stop herself, she flung her arms around him, hugging him tightly. Her heart thrilled as his arms slid solidly around her in return and gave a tight squeeze.

"I missed you." She said the words quietly enough so that he could ignore them if he wanted. He gave no reply and she reluctantly pulled back. "What are you doing here?" She gazed into his eyes, looking for a sign his hug might mean he had missed her too.

"Kate mentioned you would be home today. I thought I'd swing by to, well, to see you. We need to talk."

"Those aren't words a woman typically likes to hear. What do you want to talk about?" Fiona felt her heart speed up. Maybe this was when he'd tell her he missed her too?

"Here, move and I'll grab your stuff."

Fiona knew she had a stupid grin on her face, but right now, she didn't care. Peter Grant had missed her. Why else would he have met her just as she arrived home? It seemed as if Operation Catch a Pastor was working after all. She'd just needed to get out of his sight for a few weeks.

She grabbed her purse off the front seat and her phone out of the holder before hurrying up the stairs with Peter following. Snagging her keys from her pocket, Fiona unlocked the door. She stepped inside, holding it for him.

"Did you bring back potatoes? What do you have in here that's so heavy?" Peter dropped her bags on the floor with a grunt.

"Um, well, yeah. I went to The County. Of course, I brought back potatoes, silly! Seriously, my Gram wouldn't let me leave without some." Fiona let her laugh ring out. It was almost surreal to be standing in her kitchen chatting with Peter as if she'd never left. It was as if no time had passed between their dance rehearsals for Kate and Drew's wedding over two months ago. She prayed this wasn't a dream she would wake from.

She tucked a stray strand of fiery hair behind her ear and began pulling off her coat and gloves. "How are things going with Lucas and Bree? Is everything all set for tonight?"

"Honestly, I have no idea. I just know I'm showing up at the Three Cats at eight o'clock. I'll meet Lucas, go over what he needs to do, and we'll start the ceremony about thirty minutes later. If you want any more details than that, you'll need to talk with Bree or Kate."

Fiona laughed again. "Men!"

"Hey now, I resemble that remark."

The smile died on Fiona's lips. "Yeah, yeah you do."

Peter's smile faded. Uh oh. Her chest tightened. "What did you want to talk to me about?"

The ringing of a cell phone made Fiona jump as she felt the vibration in her hand. She glanced down to where she still had her phone clutched. The called ID said "Mom" and her mother's face smiled back at her from the screen.

Groaning, she closed her eyes. "I have to take this."

"Please do. I can wait."

Turning her back, she walked away, gathering herself before answering. Her mother had some sort of sixth sense, and Fiona didn't want to discuss Peter with her while he was in the room.

"Hey Mom, what's up? I just pulled in a few minutes ago."

"I wanted to be sure you got home okay. How was Grandma Josie when you left?"

"She was a little bummed I left even though she didn't say much. I'd been planning to stay until after Christmas, but my friends are getting married tonight."

"Tonight? And you didn't know about it?"

Fiona laughed as she watched Peter moving around her apartment. She liked having him here. His presence filled the space in a way she hadn't realized she needed.

"They were planning to be married in the spring anyway. I guess they got tired of waiting."

Her eyes met Peter's and time seemed to slow. He was looking at her so intently Fiona lost her train of thought. She realized her mother was still talking, but she had no idea what had been said.

Swallowing hard, she turned her back on Peter. "Sorry, Mom. What was that again?"

"Darling, is everything okay? You sound distracted."

Fiona held back laughter. Her mother's radar was working well. "Distracted. Yeah, just a little. Um, Mom, I've got to run. I told Bree and Kate I'd go help decorate. I'll call you tomorrow."

She barely heard her mother's response as she swiped the phone off. She turned back to Peter. "I do have to help them. I have," she glanced at her watch, "only about thirty minutes before I need to meet them at the café. What did you want to talk about?"

"It's good to have you back, Fee."

"That's nice to hear. It's good to be back."

"I've had time to think since you've been gone." Peter ran a hand through his hair.

"I was hoping you did." She gave him one of her mega-watt smiles.

"And the thing is, I think it's best if we just remain friends. I know you've wanted more and so have I at times, but it's just not good timing right now. I need to give my sole focus to Seaside."

The smile slid off Fiona's face. That wasn't what she thought he was going to say. What happened to absence making the heart grow fonder and all that nonsense? He wanted to stay friends? Not if she had anything to say about it.

"Did you hear me, Fiona?"

Fiona looked Peter in the eye as she felt her temper rising. Peter Michael Grant was about to get a good dose of it. "Oh, I heard you. I just can't believe what you just said. Try me again because I'm wondering why we spent time together before I went north. I'm wondering why you've been texting me while I've been gone. Because from where I stand, it feels like you were just playing, just leading me on. I thought we had something. I thought you were better than that. So, what's really going on, Peter?"

Fiona winced inwardly as she heard her voice rise. At least they weren't having this conversation at the wedding. Even so, he wanted this talk *before* going to the wedding? Lovely.

Peter ran a hand again through his hair and grabbed the back of his neck. Fiona wanted to grab his hair too, but not to run her fingers through it like she usually wanted to do. No, this time she wanted to grab a handful and yank it. Maybe try to shake some sense into him.

"Look, I know this isn't easy. It isn't easy for me either, Fiona."

"Really? Because right now I feel humiliated. I've been practically throwing myself at you since the wedding. Heck, even before, if I'm being honest. And it seems *one* of us should be honest here. I thought you were going to finally ask me out tonight, Peter. On a real date. Not," Fiona waved her hands around like a conductor, "do whatever it is this is."

Peter paced away from her and stood for a moment with his back turned. She wasn't sure if he had hoped she would make it easy for him, but that wasn't in her personality. She didn't shy away from confrontation. She wanted it out in the open. She hated it when people weren't honest with her so she always gave as honestly as she could because of her own need for the truth.

"You're not a priest, Peter. You're allowed a relationship. Even with my limited Bible knowledge, I know that's true. So, what's the real reason you're trying to kill this relationship before we even have a chance to see where we could go?"

Peter swung back to her, and she finally saw something more than calmness in his eyes. She saw an answering fire. Good. She was geared up for a good fight.

"I know I'm not a priest. I'm just trying to follow God here. I've been reading Paul's letters and he clearly states how it's better to be single. So, whatever this is between us, it has to stop. Now. My focus is going to be on Christ in my life and the church. I don't have time for a girlfriend. I need to chase after God and lead my congregation well."

Fiona felt the fight drain from her. How was she supposed to compete with God? She didn't even know what letters Peter was talking about, but she certainly wasn't going to ask him to explain more. She wasn't up for a sermon.

Peter gave her a wan smile and walked toward the door. "I'm sorry to do it like this, especially before Lucas and Bree's wedding, but I thought it was best."

Fiona watched as the man she loved, the one she thought had finally come to the same realization, closed the door behind himself and left. The memory brought back a flash from when the same thing happened with Hank after she'd confronted him about his lies. The past seemed determined to repeat itself.

Because whatever tonight was about, it wasn't what Peter had told her. There was something more going on. Now she needed to figure out if she was going to fight for him or let him go. She needed to figure out whether or not she was going to show Peter Grant what he was missing by not having her in his life.

Chapter 8

♥

F iona thought this night would go differently. She'd thought tonight would be romantic. She'd thought it would be a happy reunion with Peter after he realized how much he needed her in his life. The joke was on her.

"Fee, what's wrong with you? Do you feel okay?" Kate had popped up beside Fiona.

"I'm fine. Just tired."

"I'm glad you were able to get home. How's your grand-mother doing?"

"She's good. Still her old, cranky self." Fiona smiled when she said this though. She'd grown to really appreciate her grandmother over the last few weeks. Although, she wished she'd been able to figure out what was going on between Grandma Josie and her mom. She would have to make plans to go see her mom soon and see if she could get answers from her.

"You're sure everything's good?" Kate reached out a hand to Fiona's arm and squeezed. "You look more than tired."

"Peter met me almost as soon as I pulled in the driveway." Fiona hadn't intended to tell her friend what had happened.

She was still trying to figure out what to do next. Fiona's simple statement caused Kate to arch an eyebrow.

"And?"

"Have you seen us talking at all tonight?"

"Well, no, now that you mention it, but the guys have been sequestered in the kitchen almost since they got here."

"Has that stopped you from talking with Drew?" Fiona saw the smile bloom on her friend's face and felt a stab of jealousy.

Kate glanced toward the kitchens. "Well, no, it hasn't."

"Yeah. That's what I figured." Fiona gave her friend a small smile. "Anyway, I thought this was supposed to be a small gathering. There must be close to thirty people here at this point."

Fiona didn't want to talk about Peter right now. Her emotions were too close to the surface, and she wasn't sure if she'd break out sobbing or start punching the wall first.

Kate put a hand on her hip. "Don't think you have me fooled. But I'll let you change the subject for now. I think that's everyone. We should be starting... Oh no!"

Fiona looked where Kate was staring with a look of horror. Mrs. Johnson was marching down the sidewalk, straight towards the front door.

"Was she invited?" Fiona eyed the approaching figure.

"No, she wasn't. What are we going to do?" Kate glanced towards the kitchen.

Fiona was itching for a good fight. She needed something or someone to vent at as a way of releasing her pent-up frustration. She wasn't going to fight with Peter at Bree's wedding, but she didn't mind taking on Mrs. Johnson. She just needed to do it without causing a scene. She glanced at the clock. Ten minutes until they were set to begin.

Fiona squared her shoulders. "I've got it, Kate. Go make sure Bree is ready. It's almost time."

As Kate hurried away, Fiona pulled herself up to her full height. Taking a deep breath, she stepped outside. She shivered in the cold air. She was wearing a bulky sweater over a pair of skinny jeans with the legs tucked into a pair of tall boots. She loved these boots, even though they gave her another inch on what she felt was already too much height. Right now, however, she would use it to her advantage.

"Can I help you, Mrs. Johnson?"

Fee stood, blocking the door. When Bree had first started working at the café as a waitress, she'd had an unpleasant run-in with Mrs. Johnson. Then again, so had most of the town at some point. Bree laughed about it now, since it was also the day she'd met Lucas. But Fiona was not going to allow Agnes Johnson inside to ruin the wedding.

"You can move out of my way, young lady, and let me in."

"I'm afraid I can't do that." Fiona stifled the feeling of satisfaction on seeing the indignation on Mrs. Johnson's face.

"You cannot bar me from a public venue."

"It's closed to the public and after hours. This is a private event. If you have an invitation, I will certainly let you in. Otherwise, I can't allow it."

Fiona glanced over her shoulder to see if the ceremony had started yet. She wasn't going to miss anything because Mrs. Johnson was trying to gate crash. She didn't see Bree coming out of the office yet. As she turned back, her eyes caught Peter's as he turned to face the entrance. She felt her face flush and she turned fully back to Mrs. Johnson.

"Well, I never! Young lady, you will let me inside right now. It's too cold to stand out here arguing."

Fiona was done being polite. "You're right, Agnes. I would suggest you go get in your fancy Hummer parked down the block and go home. You aren't coming in, and I'm done arguing with you about it."

Spinning on her heel, Fiona walked back into the café and pulled the door closed behind her, shutting Mrs. Johnson outside. Keeping eye contact with the old woman, Fiona twisted the deadbolt to lock the door. Turning, she saw Bree just joining Lucas at the counter across from where Peter was standing.

At least another Grant brother was getting their happy ending. Her thoughts betrayed her bitterness over the unfairness of the situation. She didn't want to keep standing on the sidelines. She was ready for her happy ever after ending.

Her anger slipped as Lucas and Bree turned towards each other to say their vows. The love that shined from their faces brought tears to her own eyes.

Operation Catch a Pastor was in danger of failing. Snagging Peter's gaze as he turned to look out across the room, she narrowed her eyes at him. Their conversation wasn't done yet. Fiona was prepared to go to battle for him. She wasn't going to let him get away that easily.

Chapter 9

♥

Manny Grant punched the off button on his cell phone and set it down on the counter. It was done. He was now jobless and would soon be homeless. He was warned to not make radical changes to his life when he was young. He was taught to think things through and make sure to look at all the pros and cons, but he still hadn't been able to stop himself.

He'd been working as a civil engineer for the last few years. His supervisor had suggested he sit for the professional engineer's exam soon, which would allow him to write P.E. after his name. That would mean he finally could sign off on his own designs.

Except, he realized, he didn't want it. He'd spent the last four years learning how to design storm water systems and grade site designs so rainwater would drain correctly. He'd learned how to design retaining walls and lay out parking lots. And he realized, he found it all boring.

Manny had just left the job that paid his bills. He'd told them he was pursuing "other avenues." It seemed a bit reckless to toss everything away, but that's exactly what he was doing.

He'd just given his landlord notice he would not be renewing his lease. He'd given him a month's notice. That left Manny only a few weeks to get a plan in place before he ended up on the streets living out of his car.

Sighing, he rubbed a hand over his head, feeling the stubble that was his hair in the summer. His hair grew in thick and would hold in the heat of the summer days in Florida if he let it grow.

He leaned against his living room window, looking out over the city. He'd lived in Miami his whole life, well, from what he could remember anyway. Manny Grant hadn't been born a Grant. When he was two years old, he was found wandering the streets alone. Thankfully, he'd wandered right into the neighborhood fire station. The police and fire departments had searched for anyone missing a toddler. No one ever came forward.

He'd entered the foster system and found himself placed with the Grant family. He smiled at the thought of his parents. He had no memories of his life before the Grants took him in. There were marks on his body when he was found. Marks that suggested he'd been beaten or hurt in some way. God was good and those moments were erased from his memory. He was thankful for that.

The Grants brought him into their chaotic life full of both biological, adopted, and foster children. And miraculously, they chose him to stay and become a Grant forever.

He'd spoken to both his parents just last week. He video called them to tell them how he was already itching at the thought of sitting in a cubicle designing infrastructure for the rest of his life. He wasn't sure he could do it. But he knew how much college had cost his parents. He knew how much it had cost himself. He worked two jobs as well as had some help since he was a former foster child. Because of all that, he'd managed to graduate with no debt. It was this that now had him rethinking his entire plan.

"Manny," his mother said, "we love you no matter what you decide. If you need some time to think, why don't you head to Maine and stay with one of your brothers? I'm sure they would love to have you."

Manny had always felt slightly out of place in the family hierarchy. He had three older brothers and three older sisters. He was the baby and there were eight years between him and Peter, his oldest brother. All his brothers were on their own by the time Manny entered high school. He didn't know them as well as he would like given the age gap. He wondered if one of them *would* welcome him into their home. And what would he even do in Haven, Maine?

Walking over to where he'd started packing, he picked up his guitar and slung the strap over his shoulder. He strummed lightly as he hummed. Playing and singing often helped him focus and calmed him enough so he could figure out what to do next.

He remembered his father's words. "Manny, this is your opportunity to figure out exactly what you want to do. I pray you have a long life ahead of you. A life where you're likely to make many job changes. If engineering isn't what you want to do right now, don't do it. It will still be there if you change your mind.

Do what glorifies God. If you do that, it will guide you true throughout your life."

Manny continued to play as he thought over his father's words. He didn't know what he could do that would glorify God, but he was willing to find out. He plucked out the beginning notes of a song he'd started working on. No one in his family or even his friend circle, as small as it was, knew he dabbled in writing songs. It was a way for him to process his thoughts and emotions.

"Oh God, You are so good. You're everything to me. Your light shines bright. Show me the way everlasting."

His words died off as he continued strumming. God would show him the right path, but he needed to take the first step. He pulled the guitar from over his head, setting it aside. Picking up his phone, he took a deep breath and pulled up Peter's number. He punched the green call button and put the phone to his ear, listening to it ring.

"Hey! Peter! How are you? Look, I need a favor..."

Chapter 10

L ord, what am I going to do now?" Peter whispered the prayer as he dropped his forehead to his desk with a thunk and let out a groan.

The elders meeting he'd been postponing for far too long hadn't gone well tonight. Two of the five elders had handed in their resignations effective immediately. Peter hadn't realized Randy was moving to Bangor. Then Jesse chimed in how he needed to step down due to changes at his job.

The elder board had always been small. Seaside Chapel itself was a small congregation, with only about seventy-five members. There were more attendees in the summer, but never more than a hundred and fifty. Both Randy and Jesse were on the board when Peter had been hired. The only ones left now were Peter, Tom Foster, and Will Clark.

Tom and Will were in their 80s. Peter was sure the men stayed just to have something to do once a month. He'd always felt as if the two viewed the elder meetings as more of a social gathering than anything serious about church matters.

Peter wasn't sure what the next step would be. Who would be a good fit for elder? He started thinking through the list of men in the church. Sitting back in his office chair, he closed his eyes as he felt a headache starting.

Pushing the pain aside, he jumped to his feet and began to pace in his office. Maybe this was what God wanted for the church. He felt excitement begin to build. Tom and Will would still serve. Did he really need to replace Randy and Jesse? Going from five total elders to three shouldn't be an issue. Should it? He could still be the deciding vote if needed.

Peter contemplated the ramifications of not adding anyone to the board. He knew Will and Tom didn't have a contentious bone in their bodies. Not that Randy or Jesse did either, but both of those men would sometimes push back at Peter's ideas on where he thought the church should go or how things should be run. This might be a blessing in disguise.

Smiling, he headed towards the door. He should be praising God instead of worrying. Besides, when did worry ever do anything? He just needed to trust God with this. He'd told his congregation as much many times.

God wouldn't have allowed this to happen if He didn't want Peter to lead the church more effectively. Peter was sure of it. If he put his focus on his congregation, what could go wrong? After all, that's what he was doing. Focusing solely on the church.

He locked the door behind him and jumped into his truck parked in the lot. He cranked the heater. The temperature had dropped, and it was now hovering near freezing. The meeting had gone longer than usual once Jesse and Randy had shared their news.

Peter rubbed his hands together, wishing he'd thought to grab some gloves, and drove towards home. He'd just missed his deadline of finishing the bungalow by Christmas by only a couple of days thanks to adding in Lucas and Bree's wedding at the last minute.

He'd spent the holiday alone. Lucas and Bree had gone north for a few days to celebrate their marriage. Kate and Drew had flown south Christmas morning to spend the holiday weekend with family in Florida. Peter had stayed to finish his house. He still had some finish work to do, but it was close enough. He'd moved enough of his stuff in on New Year's Day to live comfortably until his brothers were back to help him move the rest.

Both his brothers were now married. All his sisters were married. The only unmarried one left in the family beside himself was Manny. And his younger brother wasn't even close to thirty yet, not like Peter. Yet, he had just put the kibosh on his own beginnings to what could have been a serious relationship with Fiona. Peter felt a small sigh escape at the thought of her name.

Telling Fiona the day of the wedding how he couldn't pursue a relationship had been one of the hardest things he'd had to do. He wasn't blind or stupid. He knew Fiona had been hoping for him to start dating her. Yet, he walked away. If he were being honest with himself, he was still struggling with it. Maybe, like Paul talked about in 2 Corinthians 12:7, this would be his "thorn in the flesh," something he'd need to continue to struggle with.

When Fiona had been gone for a month to help her grandmother, he'd missed her. A lot. In fact, far more than he'd thought he would. He'd caught himself scanning the sea of faces for her on Sunday mornings. He would walk to the café more often thinking he might run into her there. He even found himself going by Seascapes hoping to catch a glimpse of her through the window. And every time he did, he would get a jolt in his gut over the fact she wasn't there.

She was right, even if it was hard to admit to himself. He'd once hoped for more with Fiona. He'd imagined more than once what it would be like to have her on his arm, to introduce her as his wife. He thought often what it would be like to go home to her, after a night like this, and talk about his day. He even wondered what it might be like to kiss her a time or two.

Peter quickly stopped the way his thoughts were going. He needed to focus on what he felt the Lord had impressed on him over the last few weeks. His focus needed to be on the church and his congregation. He didn't have time to have his attention divided between that and a woman, no matter what his emotions told him.

After all, emotions lie. Proverbs 3:5-6 told him that very thing. If he kept leaning on his own understanding of life, he'd get nowhere. He thought God had shown him the path to take. Now his heart would just have to get on board with what his head knew to be true.

Peter turned his thoughts to the message he was preparing. He originally had been working through the theme of being a good steward. Now he wondered if he shouldn't switch to the theme of trust instead.

His mind continued to ponder the two choices as he drove home, deep in thought. There were so many things he needed to juggle at the church between schedules of events and visiting people both in the hospital and shut-ins at home. He often worked late into the night and rose early to try to get everything done.

He was tired of answering the phone and putting bulletins together. Peter would love help with the administrative tasks. After Mrs. Johnson had called him out on missing some hospital visits, he knew he needed to do something different. It was just a matter of finding the right person for the job.

The women's auxiliary helped on occasion, but he needed someone there on a more permanent basis. He never knew when one of the women would show up to answer the phone or do some other small administrative tasks.

He made a mental note to schedule a meeting with Judy Harris, chair of the women's auxiliary, to see if she had any idea of anyone who could work on a regular basis. Maybe he should talk with Drew about it as well since he seemed to know everyone in town. His outgoing brother had never met a stranger.

Peter pulled into the driveway and gave a start. He saw a car parked there, one he recognized. His gut clenched. What was Fiona doing here this late at night? He knew she hadn't liked what he had said Christmas Eve. He scoffed under his breath. He had enough sisters to know breakups were never easy. His brow furrowed at the thought.

It wasn't a breakup. How could it be? They'd never officially dated, but it felt like a breakup. He'd been foolish to think Fiona would just let it go, but he hated confrontations. This was the very thing he'd hoped to avoid.

He swallowed hard as he stared at her through the windshield. She was bundled up against the cold in a pair of jeans framing her long legs so well, tall boots, and an anorak with a fur collar pulled up. It framed her face, pink with cold. He held back the sigh at how beautiful she was. He was committed to following Christ. Fiona was a sister in Christ. His brain just needed time to catch up to the fact he'd placed Fiona off limits.

Peter pulled his truck forward to where he usually parked, mind now whirring. It would have been too easy to simply fall into a relationship with Fiona. After all, her best friend was married to his brother. The couples spent a lot of time together. Peter enjoyed spending time with Fiona. He even looked forward to it. She'd been right when she threw back at him how often he did just that.

Maybe things would change in the future, but for now, he didn't have time for a woman or dating or marriage. Being in a relationship would take away his focus from his main goal, devotion to Christ and his congregation.

The only problem was his head still hadn't informed his heart he no longer cared for Fiona Gilliam.

Chapter 11

♥

F iona knew she was taking a chance, but she hadn't been able to stop herself. She wasn't sure what made her drive out to Peter's house. She wasn't even sure he was living here, but a quick text to Kate earlier revealed he'd moved in a few days ago.

While she'd started thinking of Peter as more than a friend during their dance rehearsals, it was during the time of renovating his new home when she'd started to want more of a relationship with him. That was when she'd seen his humor and his heart, and she wanted both in her life.

It hadn't helped watching the other two couples share knowing glances, quick kisses, and hugs. That had only made her want the same thing. She wanted to feel love like that. She wanted to feel protected and safe. She wanted to feel like she was the most important person to someone else.

She shook off thoughts of the past. Thoughts of Hank could still make her blood boil. She'd changed far too much of herself to fit into his world only to have him betray her so completely. She'd taken a long time to realize Hank had failed her and not the other way around.

She wasn't going to get caught up in that again. She knew who she was, and now she knew who she belonged to. Being a child of God had certainly changed her perspective on life even more.

Fiona stood and began walking towards Peter's truck. She'd almost given up. Thankfully she had dressed for the cold. She wore lined jeans, a pair of old Uggs she couldn't bear to part with, an oversized wool sweater, and a parka with a lined hood pulled up.

She'd spent most of the time waiting in the car with the heater going until sleep threatened to overtake her. Sitting in the cold on the porch had at least kept her awake. She wasn't going to let Peter slip by her without a conversation, a hard conversation. She was done dancing around this, whatever this was. She knew what Peter had said. The problem was, she didn't believe him.

Too often she caught Peter looking at her, with a look a friend did not give another friend. It was the same look she saw Drew give Kate or Lucas give Bree. It was a look that meant there was more. He may have said he didn't want to date, but his expressions proved otherwise.

Fiona was sure Peter had almost kissed her once or twice as well. He'd get this look that always made her mouth go dry and her heart race. Just thinking of it now as she walked towards him had the same effect on her. She was tired of dreaming about what it would feel like to kiss the man.

She stood, trying not to tap her foot with impatience, while Peter parked the truck and turned off the lights. He didn't get out immediately. He just sat in his truck staring at her through the windshield. Yes, sitting on someone's porch for hours, waiting for them to come home, might be construed as a little stalker-ish, but she had been willing to take the chance.

Peter slowly pushed open the door and stepped out. Shutting it behind him, he moved toward her. He kept his eyes locked on hers and Fiona fought to stay focused on what she wanted to say. He had a way of making her mind go blank when he was this close.

She loved his eyes. Even if they were hard to see in just the light from the porch. She hoped they showed the same thing she was feeling. Hope. Attraction. Something more than friendship.

After all the time they'd spent practicing the dance routine, she was no closer to having Peter for her own than before. Here they were, still doing the same steps around each other. And Fiona wanted a new dance routine. One where they could share their heart with each other. Taking a deep breath, she jumped in with both feet.

"Hey." Nice, Fee. It's almost midnight, you're at this man's house, and you start with "hey." She shook her head at her foolishness yet waited for Peter to reply.

"Hey, yourself. What are you doing here? Is everything okay?"

"Of course. I...uh...I just..." Fiona's voice trailed off. Giving herself a mental shake, she stiffened her spine and started again. "I need to talk to you."

A shadow cross Peter's face. Fiona wasn't going to let him duck away from this. She was willing to fight for him and wanted him to know it.

"It's kind of late, Fiona. I'm tired. Can we do this tomorrow instead?"

"No, we need to talk now. It won't take long. I don't even need to come inside."

She heard Peter sigh and saw his shoulders slump. Maybe she should come back later. The man was obviously exhausted, but she kept quiet.

"Okay, but let's go in. It's too cold to stay outside." Peter went up the porch steps with Fiona trailing after him. He pulled open the unlocked door, and she followed him inside.

Wrapping her arms around herself, Fiona shivered. It had been cold out there, and she'd been foolish to wait so long. But she knew if she left, it would be easy to keep pushing this conversation off. She'd decided the fight for Peter's heart was worth it. He didn't know the battle had just begun.

"Can I get you something hot to drink?" Peter moved into the kitchen, flipping on light switches as he went.

"Peter!"

He turned, concern on his face.

"The place looks amazing!" The last time Fiona had been inside, the walls were still just studs. Since she'd been gone, they'd been covered in sheetrock and finished. They were painted a light beige with burnt orange accents.

She could make out a few things that still needed to be done, like molding around the windows and light covers added. But the transformation was stunning, just as she'd once predicted.

"You've really been busy! How did you get this all done?"

Peter relaxed and finished putting a kettle on to boil. "Drew and Lucas both helped and even a few men from church. It seems once they all realized I wasn't going to stay in the parsonage, they took pity on me and helped. I just have a few more finishing touches to do. And once my brothers are back from their holidays, they'll help me move the rest of my stuff in."

Fiona took in the few sparse pieces of furniture. A folding table and two metal chairs were in the kitchen area. There was a camp chair and an upended box next to it in the living room.

"So, what's so important you've been waiting on my porch all night in this cold to speak to me?"

Fiona took a deep breath and plunged in. It was now or never. "I like you. I like you a lot. I like spending time with you. The texts you sent while I was gone were the highlight of my day." She stopped before she started repeating herself. She risked a quick look to see if Peter was giving off any type of reaction to her confession.

He was leaning against the counter, his eyes focused on the floor. His hands were shoved in the pockets of his jeans. He didn't raise his head.

Well, she thought to herself, this is awkward. Time to step it up, Fee.

She'd said what she'd come to say. She had more, but she was going to wait to see how Peter reacted to this confession.

"Fee," Peter's voice broke as he looked up at her, but he didn't move and neither did Fiona. She caught a glimpse of pain in his eyes before he looked away.

Peter cleared his throat and tried again, "Fiona, I wish things could be different. I really do, but I can't, no, I won't be involved with you or anyone. Tonight, some things happened that confirmed that for me. The church needs to be first for me. It's going to be my focus. I don't have time for a relationship with anyone other than God."

Fiona swallowed hard. She wasn't sure what she'd hoped to accomplish tonight. No, that wasn't right. She'd hoped Peter would realize the mistake he'd made and choose her.

Peter cleared his throat again. "I don't want to muddle things here. I enjoy your friendship. It's impossible to avoid each other given how small Haven is or Kate and Drew's marriage. I hope we can be civil to each other. Friends?"

Fiona couldn't look at him. She felt her temper rising. Soon it would be to the point where she wouldn't be able to hold back her tongue. Her mother had always warned her to get a handle on it. "I should go..." She started towards the front door.

"Wait..."

Fiona stood with her back to Peter, arms crossed. Why did she always seem to give her heart away to men who didn't appreciate it?

"Fiona, I really want to be your friend. Can we do that?"

Fiona wanted to tell him to shut up. No, she didn't want to be his friend. She wanted more. How could the man be so dense? She needed to leave before she said something she would regret.

Without turning around, she said, with voice shaking, "Peter, you're so oblivious. I don't want your friendship. I want more."

She hurried to the door and yanked it open. She ran down the stairs to her car. Pulling open the door, she slipped inside.

"Fiona!"

She heard Peter calling her name, but she knew if she stopped now, she would say something she'd regret.

Fiona threw the car into gear. Gravel spun under the tires as she backed up and turned around. She headed towards the road and the safety of home.

Glancing in the rearview mirror just before she pulled out onto the street, Fiona saw Peter standing on the porch watching her. Friends. She wasn't sure her heart could take being put in the friend-zone by a man she loved. And she did love Peter Grant. She just needed to figure out a way to show him.

Chapter 12

♥

K ate Grant squeezed her husband's hand as they sat together in the doctor's office. She glanced over at Drew, thankful all over again for having him in her life and, most importantly, marrying him last fall. They were only three months out from their wedding and still acting like newlyweds. She just couldn't help herself.

Drew turned his head and their eyes caught. "Doing okay?"

Kate nodded, "Yeah. Just eager to hear." She felt herself calm when he squeezed her hand.

There was a knock on the door just before the doctor opened it. Kate scanned Doctor Adams's face, looking for any sign as to what the results would be.

The doctor wasted no time. With a large grin she said, "Congratulations! You're pregnant!"

Drew gave a shout of joy and Kate was lifted out of her chair into his arms for a hug. She buried her face in his neck and laughed with delight.

The doctor laughed along with the couple. "We're going to get you set up with your next appointment. We'll want to see you monthly to start. Here's a prescription for prenatal vitamins. You should start taking them daily. Do you have any questions?"

Drew released Kate and extended his hand to the doctor. "Thanks, Doctor Adams."

The doctor took his hand and shook it. "Well, all I did was deliver the news! Based on the information you gave me, I put you at about eight weeks pregnant. You've got about 32 weeks ahead of you. You're due in early June."

Kate's heart squeezed with happiness as she saw Drew grinning foolishly at her. She tried to pay attention as Doctor Adams continued to give them instructions. She reached for Drew's hand as they left the exam room. Kate's other hand went to her stomach in a protective gesture. A baby. She was going to be a mom.

Her smile slipped as she remembered her own mother and her chaotic childhood. It hadn't been happy. Not in the least. Her mother's mental illness caused the death of her younger sister and resulted in Kate being placed in foster care for years until her father finally showed up and claimed her. It hadn't improved her circumstances though. Her life with her father had been anything but happy or stable.

Looking back on her life now, Kate was thankful. The same family that had adopted Drew after his parents were killed in a car accident had once been Kate's foster family. She'd been back with her father by the time Drew came to live with the Grant family.

The Grants had been all ready to adopt her when her father showed up out of the blue and reclaimed his rights to her. He'd whisked her away from a stable family to a life where she'd been neglected by her alcoholic parent.

As she looked at her husband, she was overcome with the gratitude for God's plan in her life. He had made all things good for her, even through the pain of her childhood. She was now looking forward to the coming joy of having her own child.

As they walked out to the parking lot, Drew placed a hand on the back of Kate's neck and squeezed gently. "It's going to be okay, Kate. You're going to be a great mother. Don't worry, sweetheart."

Kate shook off thoughts of her childhood. She'd spent too long in therapy working out her issues to let them all derail her now at the thought of becoming a mother. It would be okay. She had Drew by her side. Her father was now sober. He would be excited to hear about his first grandchild. And the Grants would be thrilled to add another to their side as well.

She waited as Drew opened the door of his truck for her and helped her in. He was already starting to treat her as if she was delicate. "You know, I'm not going to break, right? Women have been having babies for centuries. They used to work right up until the point they went into labor. Then they would squat in the field and just pop them right out into the dirt before going straight back to work."

Kate held back laughter as she watched Drew's eyes grow wide. He gave an exaggerated shudder. "True. But none of them were having my baby." He leaned forward and kissed her, slowly and sweetly. "I already love him or her and you most of all." He gave her one last kiss on the forehead before shutting her door carefully and jogging around the front to climb in.

Kate was still amazed she was married to such a loving man. And now she would soon be a mother. Once more she hoped she would be the mother this child needed. She wrapped her arms around her middle. She knew that, unlike her mother, she would never harm her baby.

She missed her sister, Lori. The younger sister she barely remembered. The one who had died when Kate was five and Lori was only two years old due to their mother's mental illness.

She stopped. Lori. "What do you think of the name Lori if it's a girl?"

"I think it's perfect." Drew reached across the center console and squeezed her hand. He continued holding it as he pulled onto the street. "Do you want to go see your dad and let him know in person?"

"Yeah. I want to tell him without an audience around. We should invite everyone else over for lunch after church on Sunday. We can tell them all together. Do you think you can hold it together that long without calling your brothers?"

Drew laughed. "Doubtful, but I can try. What about doing a video call with my parents tonight to let them know?" He lifted their clasped hands and kissed the back of hers.

"We can do that," Kate laughed. Her free hand drifted once more to cover her still flat stomach. It was hard to believe there was a child growing inside her. A fierce protectiveness filled her. She would protect this child, like a mama bear. Nothing would ever harm him or her, not if there was anything she could do about it.

She felt a squeeze of her hand again and looked at her husband. "It's going to be okay," Drew said once more. "You've got me, and I won't let anything hurt our little one."

She smiled as his words echoed her thoughts. They were in this together. Even as tears filled her eyes, she held her smile at Drew. God had so blessed her with this man. And the blessings continued with the growing life inside her.

Chapter 13

♥

A men." Peter opened his eyes and looked out over the congregation. As Drew led the worship team back on to the stage to close out the morning, Peter slipped down the side. He walked towards the back of the church, so he'd be ready to greet people as they left.

A headache was beginning to throb at the front of his head. He had already been cornered by the women's auxiliary before church had even started this morning. He also needed to speak with Drew about some needed repairs. The old building seemed to need more maintenance lately. As much as he loved running his church, today he wished he could slip away and walk the beach until the calmness he was missing filled him.

He was looking forward to lunch with Drew and Kate. The brothers often gathered on Sunday, but Drew made a point to make sure Peter was coming today. And soon Manny would be with them as well.

His youngest brother was taking a few weeks to make his way north. He was going to move in with Peter for a little while. Manny said he needed to figure out a new direction in life, that engineering wasn't working for him. Peter was looking forward to getting to know his youngest brother better.

Bringing his thoughts back to today, Peter wondered how lunch might go. He wanted to ask Drew if Fiona was coming. He almost blushed at the thought of sitting across from her. He hadn't wanted to give his brother the idea that it mattered. It didn't. Not really.

He felt the quick nudge in his spirit at the lie. If he was being honest, he had wanted to wrap his arms around Fiona and kiss her senseless last night. He shook the thought away. It wasn't productive. He'd made his choice and would live with it until God made it clear things should change.

Sighing, Peter plastered on a smile and waited as the worship band wrapped up their song. As the last notes faded, Peter listened as Drew said the final prayer. "Lord, thank You. Thank You for being holy. For You are holy. Holy and merciful. Thank You for Your mercy and grace. We don't deserve either and yet You pour out both abundantly on us when we simply ask. Be with us as we leave this place today. Keep us safe until we once more come together to worship You next week. Amen."

Peter raised his head and watched as his brother led the band in an instrumental version of the song they'd just sung together. A quiet hum of voices added to the music as people began to gather their belongings. A mother chased a child, and someone woke up old Cecil Barrett.

"That was a wonderful sermon, Pastor Peter. Well done. Please pray for my sister, Hazel. She's feeling a bit under the weather lately."

Peter smiled and nodded as Judy Harris shook his hand. She was the head of the women's auxiliary this year. He knew he should be paying closer attention to the congregation as they left, but his mind was on other things. What if Fiona came to lunch this afternoon? And why wouldn't she? She always had in the past. How awkward would it be? Would she even talk to him or just ignore him?

Peter smiled reflexively as he continued to greet everyone as they left. He tuned out the shrieks of children trying to pelt each other with handfuls of snow that wouldn't hold together. Men hurried home so they could sit on the couch, watch football, and relax before starting a busy work week. Women gathered children like protective hens, herding them toward vehicles.

Feeling lonely at the sight of all the family groups, Peter reached to shake the last hand and found himself face to face with Agnes Johnson. He groaned inwardly before beginning to pray fervently that the woman wouldn't have any complaints today. He knew it was a futile wish. Agnes Johnson always had complaints. He just didn't have the energy to placate the elderly woman. Not today.

"Good afternoon, Mrs. Johnson. Thank you for coming. Have a great week." Peter hoped the sentiment would help push her along. The woman stood a little taller and he knew the good Lord was not going to grant him that bit of mercy today.

"Young man! We need to talk. What is this I hear about Randy and Jesse leaving? There is absolutely no way Tom and Will can help you run this church. I think it's time you considered appointing some deaconesses. It's time to let the women of this church help lead. You know we'll do a better job of it."

Peter's back bristled. They were back to the same old argument. He'd lost track of the number of times Mrs. Johnson had pushed for this. He prayed silently for mercy in his response.

He took a deep breath. "Mrs. Johnson, I want to remind you that we are an elder led church. We do not have deacons. We do not have deaconesses. Tom, Will, and I will be just fine for a little while. We'll be talking about how to proceed now that Randy and Jesse are leaving. For now, please pray for the Lord to grant us wisdom so we'll make the right choices." Peter hoped this would be enough to deter her from discussing the matter further.

"Well! That's ridiculous. First Baptist has elders, deacons, and even deaconesses plus an entire board of trustees."

Apparently, it was not going to be enough. Peter held back his sigh and made sure to keep a neutral expression on his face. "Seaside Chapel and First Baptist are different. Now, I must go find someone I need to speak with before they leave. You have a good day, Mrs. Johnson."

Mrs. Johnson fumed. "We'll see about that!" She sniffed, tossed her head high, and marched out the door.

Peter quickly shut the door behind her and locked it. He walked to his office, shutting off lights as he went. He knew he should probably be worried about Mrs. Johnson's parting words, but today he just wanted to *not* worry about the church for a little while.

He stopped in the middle of the sanctuary, closed his eyes, and breathed deeply. He always enjoyed standing right here and feeling like he was in the presence of the Lord. Sometimes the feeling was more prominent. It often helped him get his mind refocused, like now. He needed to remember that he was doing this all for God and no one else. Not Mrs. Johnson. Not even himself. Just the Lord.

Agnes Johnson always made sure everyone knew her opinion. She thought she was always right and seemed to work to make those around her miserable. Peter sighed as he continued to make his way towards his office. "God, help me see her through your eyes." He often prayed those words when there was someone who rubbed him the wrong way. He knew Mrs. Johnson had a good heart. She was a child of God after all, a sister in the faith. But there were times when he wished he could, well, he didn't know what. He just knew he was getting tired of dealing with the likes of Agnes Johnson.

He grabbed his keys and walked out the back door, pulling it tight behind him. Once more Peter's thoughts drifted back to Fiona. Again. He hadn't seen her in church today. He hoped she wasn't skipping just to avoid him. He didn't want that.

As he backed out of his parking spot, he prayed Fiona would be at Drew and Kate's. After all, that's what a good pastor would do. He should pray for one of his members who hadn't been in church that day.

But for the life of him, he couldn't remember anyone else who had been missing. Just the vivacious redhead he was hoping he would still see today. He needed to have a stern talk with his heart and remind it that women, in particular Fiona Gilliam, were off limits. He was going to stay single, just as Paul suggested, so he would be able to walk a life worthy of God. That was his only desire.

He prayed his heart could accept it.

Chapter 14

♥

Fiona stood at the island in the middle of Kate and Drew's kitchen trying hard to appear casual without being obvious she was waiting for Peter to arrive. She'd skipped church this morning. After spending the night tossing and turning, she'd turned her alarm off and gone back to sleep. She'd had just enough time to shower and make it to lunch. If Kate hadn't told her how important it was for her to be here, she would have begged off.

She wasn't going to avoid Peter. Oh no, not at all. She just needed to rethink Operation Catch a Pastor. The man didn't know what was right in front of him, and she was going to show him exactly what he would be missing if he stuck to this silly edict he had come up with.

She just needed to figure out how to play it today. Would she be cool, pretending everything was fine? Act like they were friends and friends only? Try again to convince Peter to date her?

Fiona knew she didn't match the typical pastor's wife. At least not what she thought a pastor's wife should be. She was loud and opinionated. There was nothing meek or mild about her. She doubted there ever would be.

And there was still so much she needed to learn. Biblical verses and passages she should memorize. Books she should read. Things she should just know but didn't. She didn't even know how to download all that information into her brain at a rapid enough pace that it would make a difference. All she could do was be herself. That would have to be enough.

Kate had been the driving force behind Fiona finally choosing God. Fiona had always said she didn't need anyone, not even God. She was happy with herself. It had taken her years to get to that point.

Fiona knew how her ex-boyfriend's betrayal had destroyed her confidence for a while. It had taken her time after Hank to find her way back to herself. She shook off thoughts of the past and decided enough was enough. She didn't need anyone else to give her worth. She would never again change who she was to please anyone.

It wasn't like she hadn't believe in God. Fiona had always thought there was something or someone up there, but she'd never given it more of a thought than that. She hadn't cared to really. Her life had always seemed fine to her.

That was before Kate had shown her what it meant to live for Christ. To truly live her life based on what God thought of her rather than worrying about what anyone else thought of her. It had been hard to accept. She was so unworthy of Christ's mercy, but Kate had shown her that was *exactly* the point. They were all just sinners saved by grace, God's grace.

Fiona realized she often acted loud and boisterous to hide the fact she was unsure at times. It had been a hard truth to swallow. The knowledge had helped her become more of the person she wanted to be in every situation. For that, she was thankful.

Kate had started meeting with Fiona on a weekly basis to discuss the Bible. Bree also joined them. Fiona enjoyed her time with Bree and Kate. All of them were rather new at learning what it meant to read the Bible and live it out.

"He's coming. Don't worry." Fiona startled as she felt a hand on her shoulder. Kate scooted past her to get a bowl of potato salad from the fridge. "Church was busier than usual today. Here, make yourself useful and go put this on the table."

"I don't know what you're talking about. Marriage has addled your brain." Fee grabbed the bowl and walked to the table. She prayed the slight blush starting to bloom on her cheeks would be gone by the time she turned back around.

As Fiona placed the bowl on the table, she heard tires crunching on the gravel outside, and her head shot up. Kate had been right. Peter's truck was pulling into the yard. The man she couldn't seem to stop thinking about was here.

Get it together, Fee. Don't embarrass yourself. Tone it down. Just act casual. She continued the running words of encouragement to herself as she tried to stop her hands from smoothing her hair or clothes. He just wanted to be friends. She could do that. She could. Until she finally showed him how much better it could be if they were a couple.

She knew Kate was watching her. Fiona still hadn't told her what happened before Bree and Lucas's wedding. And she certainly hadn't told Kate about her confrontation with the man just a few days ago.

She jumped as she felt a hand grab hers. She turned to see Kate standing beside her with a wry smile on her face. "Just be yourself. The two of you just need to get out of each other's way. Stop trying so hard. Just be you."

"That's not working." Fee regretted her Irish heritage. She knew a blush was stealing over her cheeks. There was no hiding anything from Kate. There never was. "We're only ever going to be just friends. Nothing more."

"Keep telling yourself that." Kate laughed as she tugged on her friend's hand. "Come on. Let's go check on how the guys are doing getting those burgers grilled."

The women walked outside. The day was one of those perfect winter days when it was warm enough to give hope that spring was coming. The January thaw was upon them, and Fiona was glad.

She had on her comfortable Uggs and an oversized sweater over a pair of lined leggings. She didn't even need a jacket today. Drew and his brothers were standing just outside the garage by the grill laughing together. Smoke drifted down the driveway.

"Just in time!" Drew pulled his wife into a short embrace.

"Get a room!" Lucas called from where he stood with Bree in front of him with his arms wrapped around her.

Fiona had enjoyed getting to know Bree since she'd joined their group just last year. She'd shown up in Haven and stayed. Lucas had rescued her from a stalker, and they had fallen in love along the way. And now they were married.

"Hey, I'll hug my wife anytime I want to. Now, help me get these burgers inside so we can eat!" Drew tapped Lucas on the shoulder with a fist and the two men started loading the burgers, onions, and mushrooms on plates to bring in.

Fiona avoided meeting Peter's eyes. She was still trying to figure out if she should confront him again or if that would make him leave. She didn't want him to leave.

"Hi, Fiona," Peter said as he walked toward her. "I saw you weren't in church this morning. Everything okay?"

"Oh, um, I overslept. I'll be there next week." Fee sped up slightly to get ahead of Peter as her face began to heat. She was starting to feel like a teenager again. Why couldn't she act her age? She would be turning twenty-nine in February. She needed to stop blushing every time the man looked at her.

This was silly. She wanted the man, and she was a grown woman. She needed to get her emotions under control as well as the situation. Peter didn't know it yet, but he was going to fall in love with her. Firming her shoulders, she walked inside, glancing back to see how close Peter was to her. She whipped her head back around when she saw he was right behind her.

Inside the group quickly set up the food buffet style and fixed plates. They jockeyed for the food and joked with each other as only close friends do. It was starting to feel a little awkward to be in a group with only couples. It made it even more obvious that Peter and Fiona were not a couple.

They were soon seated at the table and Fiona found herself directly across from Peter. Good. She could work with this.

Fiona's thoughts once more went to Hank North, her ex-fiancé, that had been trying to find leverage in her brain for days. She was too tired to shove them to the back where they belonged.

They'd been a serious couple about six years ago. Hank came from money, and she'd been easily swept up in the high-profile life he led. She hadn't hesitated to accept his proposal when it had come. Her only goal in life had been to be a wife and mother. She'd thought Hank was the man to make that dream a reality.

She succeeded in pushing the memories to the back of her mind. Dwelling on the past wasn't going to change anything. It was becoming clear that maybe she just wasn't wife material. Hank had shown he didn't really want her. Not really. And now Peter had stated he was going to remain single. Fiona was beginning to wonder if the Lord might have the same plans for her.

"Can I get everyone's attention please?" Drew smiled at his wife as he made the announcement.

Fiona's focus returned as Drew stood at the head of the table.

Lucas and Peter continued to chat, not having noticed Drew.

Drew tried again, "Hey, lug heads! Listen up!"

Still the men continued to talk, brows intent on whatever they were discussing.

Suddenly a roll came flying down the table and smacked Peter on the head.

"Hey!" Peter whirled to glare down the table at Drew. "Why'd you do that?"

Drew smirked at his brother. "Because you two wouldn't stop talking. Now listen up. I have an announcement to make."

Bree, Kate, and even Fiona laughed at the antics of the brothers. Peter continued to glare at Drew while Lucas snagged the roll that had fallen to the table. He made to throw it back at Drew but stopped when Drew gave him a stern look.

"As you all know, my lovely wife and I are newly married."

"You don't say," Lucas drawled as he started eating the roll Drew had tossed at Peter. "You do know that you've been married longer than I have, right?"

Drew ignored his brother and continued. "But we've decided we need a change."

That statement got everyone's attention. Fiona gave Kate a look of concern, but her friend was smiling. She turned her attention back to Drew.

"What do you mean by change?" Peter looked at them, worry scrunching his forehead.

"Wipe those frown lines off your face, brother. Kate and I have decided we need a change in the number of people living here."

"I'm not moving back in. Don't even ask." Lucas took a large bite of the roll and raised an eyebrow at his brother. "I like my new living arrangements just fine." Lucas leaned over to brush a kiss on Bree's cheek.

"No, trust me. I don't want that either. No, Kate and I had something else in mind. We just don't know exactly who the person will be at the moment."

"Sounds sketchy to me." Peter snagged the other piece of roll from Lucas's plate and took a bite, never taking his eyes off Drew.

Fee caught Kate's eyes and knew in that moment what was going on. She squealed and clapped her hands. "Yes!"

"Yes, what?" Lucas looked at her in confusion.

"Don't steal my thunder, Fee. Let's see if these knuckleheads can figure this out." Drew's grin widened as he continued. "Kate and I decided we will be going from two to three people living here in, oh, about seven months."

Fiona jumped up and ran around to where Kate was sitting and pulled her into a hug. "I'm so happy! I'm going to be an auntie!"

Understanding soon followed as the rest of the room figured out what Drew meant. Congratulations and whoops of happiness echoed throughout the room. Fiona's eyes caught Peter's, and her smile faded as she wondered what it would be like if it were the two of them making the announcement. And she began blushing all over again.

Chapter 15

♥

P eter leaned back in his chair as he observed the young woman sitting across from him. If he had to guess, Kelsey James was in her mid-twenties. She had shoulder length, slightly wavy, blonde hair, and pale blue eyes. His eyes flicked quickly to take in the rest of her. As a pastor, there was nothing worse than getting caught in anything that might be taken, correctly or not, as checking out a woman. He determined she was pretty, but not as pretty as a certain redhead. He brought his focus back to the woman sitting in front of him.

Kelsey had come highly recommended by Mrs. Harris for the position of church secretary. Judy Harris was related to Kelsey in some way. He knew all the women on the auxiliary were strongly advocating for her to be hired, even Mrs. Johnson. Normally that would make him cautious, but he was desperate for help. He hoped Kelsey would be a good fit. He didn't want to face the auxiliary if he decided not to hire her.

"So, Kelsey, tell me why you want this position?"

"I'm burned out, honestly."

He raised an eyebrow at her. How could this young twenty-something be feeling burned out? She had barely started living. He hoped his thoughts hadn't just come across his face, but he was feeling a bit cynical at the answer. "Care to elaborate on that?" He knew something about feeling burned out. He really should take a vacation soon.

"I graduated with a degree in business, which I completed in three years. That in and of itself was intensive. I immediately took a job in Boston at a large acquisitions firm. It was cut-throat." Kelsey stopped and cleared her throat before taking a sip from the water bottle she held.

"Turns out that when you're young, blonde, and female, you're fair game in the corporate world. Or at least some of my male co-workers thought so. I got tired of fighting off inappropriate advances and trying to claw my way up the corporate ladder. Some of my fellow female workers told me there were faster ways up the ladder if I just loosened up and didn't rebuff unwanted advances. I decided I wanted out. So, here I am, looking to re-invent myself."

God once more taught Peter how he sometimes judged too fast. "I can see how that would be difficult." He cleared his throat and shuffled the papers in front of him, trying to appear as if he was giving the issue more thought.

He knew he should go home and pray about this before doing anything rash. After all, he had committed to following God's lead in all things.

Peter gave a quick glance at the list of names still left to interview. He decided to be impulsive for once and prayed he wouldn't regret it.

"Do our hours work for you? They will be nine to three, four days a week. I can't offer benefits, but there is some flexibility to the schedule."

"It's perfect, actually. When Aunt Judy told me about the opening here, I knew it would work. I was already planning to take a step back from business and explore my options. The hours will allow me to do just that. I'm not sure what else I want to do, but the salary here will at least pay my expenses. Aunt Judy is letting me live with her for a few months. It will be enough to get by until I figure out what else I might want to do."

"Does that mean you're going to be here only a few months and then take off on me?" Peter didn't want to have to go through this process again soon.

"No, I'll commit to one year. Does that sound fair? I may stay on after that depending on what else I figure out in my life, but I think a year is what I'll need. Who knows, maybe I'll like it here too much to leave."

Kelsey gave Peter a warm smile, and he had a moment of hesitation. Was it wise to have such a lovely young woman working with him alone each day? He shook off the thought. He was just feeling older than his years. This woman would likely think his 32 years ancient.

He rose and extended his hand. "Well, welcome to Seaside Chapel, Kelsey. Can you start on Tuesday?"

"I can." Kelsey rose quickly and held out a hand to shake Peter's. "Thank you, Pastor. I look forward to working with you."

After Kelsey left, Peter prayed he hadn't made a mistake in hiring her. If anything, Kelsey was overqualified for the position, but he didn't want to spend time interviewing other candidates. The auxiliary would certainly be happy for once with his decision.

Glancing at the clock, he realized he only had a few hours before the new cleaning lady came in to talk to him about her schedule. Randy's wife had been the one who had kept the church clean and tidy. With their upcoming move to Bangor, they needed to find someone to take it over. When Judy Harris had spoken to him about Kelsey, she also mentioned Leeann Roberts was interested in cleaning the church on a regular basis.

Leeann had just started attending Seaside a few weeks ago. She was a single mom, new to the area, who was looking for some work to help supplement her income. Peter didn't know the full back story, but he trusted the auxiliary in their suggestion. He would be meeting with Leeann that afternoon to give her a run down on what needed to be done.

"Lord," Peter said out loud, "you've done it again, as usual. Maybe this time I'll remember that You always do. Thank you for bringing Kelsey and Leeann into my life. May their presence here be a blessing to all and especially to me so that I can continue to focus on You and bringing Your word to Your people here at Seaside. I can tell you have it completely in hand. Thank you, Lord, as usual." Peter stood, snagged his jacket from where he had draped it over a chair in the corner, and walked out the door. He was feeling like things were starting to come together at the church. He had a few shut-ins to visit before Leeann would be in.

"And just where do you think you're going in the middle of the day, young man?"

Peter groaned inwardly. He'd been so focused on his to-do list that he hadn't heard Mrs. Johnson come in through the door. The blast of cold air should have given him warning, but he'd assumed it was from Kelsey leaving.

"I'm just going out to do some visitations. Would you like to join me?" Peter's eyes widened slightly at the question. His brain had gotten in front of his mouth. He began to pray the woman would say no. Spending an afternoon visiting people at the hospital and nursing homes with Mrs. Johnson was not his idea of fun.

"No, but thank you for asking."

The furrow lessened from Mrs. Johnson's brow. Hmmm, maybe the old woman was just lonely. It looked as if she appreciated the invitation even if, thankfully, she hadn't taken Peter up on it.

"What can I do for you today, Mrs. Johnson?"

"Did you hire the girl?"

"What girl?" Peter held back his grin. Maybe he shouldn't tease, but he was in a good mood at having found a secretary to help with his workload.

"Don't be difficult, young man. Did you hire Judy's niece?"

"I did."

"Good. Very good."

"Anything else?"

"Make sure you hire Leeann Roberts as well, young man. Lord knows you need the help around here."

Peter's mouth dropped open as Mrs. Johnson spun on her heel and walked back out. He snapped his mouth closed. If he didn't know better, he would have thought she had come in looking for a fight and was disappointed not to have found one. Interesting.

Chapter 16

♥

Operation Catch a Pastor was in motion. Fiona knew the name was silly. She'd even shortened it to OCaP in her head. She hadn't shared it with anyone, but it made her smile every time she thought of it.

Fiona had spent time diving into the Bible itself to find where it said pastors shouldn't marry. To her eyes, the verses Peter quoted weren't about not marrying, it was about making God first whether married or not.

She needed to change his mind. She knew it might be a hard task, but hadn't Kate said to be herself? She would do just that and hope it would open his eyes to the potential for a relationship with her.

Fiona's dream had always been to be a wife and mother. Lately, that dream had featured Peter front and center.

The only hesitation she felt in moving forward was about her own qualifications to be a pastor's wife. That wasn't going to stop her from working on getting Peter to change his mind. Fiona had never let an obstacle get in her way. Her mother had always said "stubborn" was her middle name.

Sighing, she stood staring out the front window of Seascapes to the ocean across the street. It was high tide on this mid-January day. The waves were crashing along the shoreline. She knew it was cold out there. The thaw they had enjoyed last week was now over.

Fiona should be working on updating the window display for Valentine's Day, but she couldn't seem to keep herself focused on the task. Her mind kept going back to figuring out what her first step should be. She needed a foolproof plan. She needed a way to be able to show Peter what he was missing by not having her in his life more fully.

After all, marriage was her end goal. It always had been. Some women might dream of becoming a lawyer or a doctor, or having some type of career, but not Fiona. She wanted the white picket fence and the two point five kids. She always had. Working for Kate was just a stop along the way. What she really wanted to do was stay home to raise her family and take care of her home and husband. Nothing more than that. Just a simple life.

She was learning so much studying the Bible. She used to think her worth was tied to who she was and what she could accomplish, but no more. She now knew her worth was in Christ. She had read about it again just today in Ephesians. She was working on memorizing it. She quietly whispered the words out loud, "But God, being rich in mercy, because of His great love with which He loved us, even when we were dead in our transgressions, made us alive together with Christ (by grace you have been saved), and raised us up with Him, and seated us with Him in the heavenly places in Christ Jesus, so that in the ages to come He might show the surpassing riches of His grace in kindness toward us in Christ Jesus." It was comforting to know that. Even though she was a sinner, she was saved by grace. That brought a smile to her face and comfort to her soul.

Her first step in OCaP was to volunteer for the new mentoring program the town was starting called Community Cares. They would be matching mentors with at-risk children. She figured the best way to show Peter she was capable of being a pastor's wife was to volunteer for things like this in the community.

Maybe she should join the women's auxiliary as well. Although, having to deal with Mrs. Johnson on a regular basis made her pause. She gave herself a mental kick. Fiona knew she would have to deal with people like Mrs. Johnson on a regular basis if she were ever to become a pastor's wife. She would talk to Judy Harris soon about joining. The more she could show Peter she could handle the duties of a pastor's wife, the better for her plan.

Fiona gave up on finishing the window display. She went over to the counter and picked up the flyer about the Community Cares program. She looked once more at the requirements the mentors needed to be considered.

They needed to be part of their community. Check. She worked at Seascapes and helped at the animal shelter once a month, which was dangerous since she couldn't have any animals at her apartment. She always wanted to sneak a kitten or a puppy out with her every time she went. Volunteering allowed her to get her baby animal fix without commitment.

She needed to be able to give two hours a week to the child she would be matched with once the application process was completed. Check. She worked full-time at Seascapes but had plenty of time in the evenings and on weekends.

Fiona began to feel excitement build at the thought of being part of a young girl's life. She thought of the things they could do. She would teach her how to make jewelry. They would walk the beach searching for sea glass. She would even bring her to the animal shelter to play with the kittens.

She began to fill out the attached application. If she could finish it now, she could swing by the town office and drop it off at lunch. She turned when she heard Kate enter from the back room.

"Any chance I can convince you to run to Three Cats this morning? Munch is hungry." Kate walked towards the front as she rubbed her still flat stomach.

"You know, I'm not sure you can blame the baby just yet for your increased appetite." Fiona smiled at her friend. She was happy for Kate and Drew even though there were small feelings of jealousy she had to keep tamping down.

"And I'm just as sure I *can*. I'm dying for a hand pie, raspberry, frosted." Kate closed her eyes and licked her lips. She nodded and opened her eyes. "Yup, that's exactly what Munch says she wants, a frosted raspberry hand pie, hot out of the oven."

"She? Did you find out the sex of the baby and not tell me? I wanted to do a gender reveal party!"

"No, just intuition. And no party. We're going to wait until the baby is born to find out the sex."

"That's a little old-fashioned don't you think? Gender parties are all the rage these days. I had a few good ideas lined up already."

"Maybe, but I like the thought of meeting my child for the first time and having to figure each other out from the day they're born."

"I never thought about it that way. But what's with this 'Munch' name? Please tell me that's not what you're going to call this poor child." Fiona gave her friend a stern look.

Kate laughed. "What? Gosh no. But we need to call the baby something. Since we don't know if it's a boy or a girl, I just started calling her Munch. I have no idea why, but it seems to fit. All I want to do these days is munch on something!" Kate shrugged her shoulders and gave a wry laugh. "So... about that hand pie?"

"You got it. Anything else? Coffee?"

"No, the doctor said to lay off caffeine. I have some herbal tea out back. I'll have that ready by the time you get back. Hurry, Munch is *starving!*"

Fiona laughed as she made for the back door so she could grab her purse and jacket. It was going to be an interesting few months if the baby was already demanding food.

Fee hurried down the sidewalk clutching the bakery bag. There had been a rush at the café. Apparently, there was an out of state power crew in town heading back home after fixing some damage left by a winter storm further north. She hadn't really paid attention, but they'd all been at the Three Cats.

She thought she was going to have to wrestle one guy for the last frosted raspberry hand pie. When she told him it was for a pregnant woman with a craving, he'd backed away, hands held high. "Take it. I don't want to bring down the wrath of a pregnant lady. My wife was a monster when she didn't get her cravings. Here," he said as he reached for his wallet, "I'll even pay."

With the hard-won hand pie in her possession, plus one for herself, she made her way back to the store. Her cup of coffee was clutched in one hand and the bakery bag in the other. She didn't want to keep Munch or Kate waiting any longer for the requested confection.

Pushing open the front door, she stepped inside the shop and stopped. Kate was crying. And one look told her Mrs. Johnson was the cause.

"Young lady, enough with the theatrics. I'm simply telling you that you should think before you put new merchandise in your store. This is not a bookstore after all. You'd think you'd want my business advice."

Mrs. Johnson must be miffed about the new items that had just been put up that very day. Seascapes had always had an eclectic style. Kate and Fiona made sea glass jewelry. They contracted with other local artisans for things like pottery, driftwood sculptures, photography, artwork, and the like. Everything was made by people in Haven or the surrounding area. They had recently been approached by a local woman who had started writing books asking if they might be interested in selling some at the store. As always, they found a place for them. The books had literally been on display for maybe an hour. Now this.

"Enough!" Fiona felt the heat rising in her veins and knew her face was turning red. Her fair complexion did little to hide her emotions. And right now, she didn't care. She hadn't been this angry, this fast, in a long time. "Mrs. Johnson, I'll say this just once. Listen carefully. You will stop this nonsense right now. This isn't your store. You don't get to tell Kate how she runs it. You have no place here other than that of a customer. If you aren't here to buy something, leave. Now." Fiona was proud of how she kept her voice level, but firm.

"Well, I never!"

"That's right. You've never once thought of anyone but yourself. You've never thought what your careless words do to others. Can't you see how much you've upset Kate? She's pregnant, for goodness sake! You're standing there making a pregnant woman cry over something you have nothing to do with! Now get out!"

Fiona's voice rose as she continued. So much for keeping control. She hurried over to pull her friend close while she glared at Mrs. Johnson. "Don't make me say it again."

With a great sniff and a turn of her head, Mrs. Johnson marched toward the front of the store. Stopping at the door, she turned back. "I was just trying to help. Far be it from me to stay and give my advice if it's not wanted. But I thought Christian women like yourselves would want the truth." With that, she opened the door and swept out.

Fiona pushed away the niggle of guilt she felt at Mrs. Johnson's words and turned to Kate. "Are you okay? I can go chase her down and beat her up for you."

Kate gave a small laugh. "No, it's okay. It's just pregnancy hormones. I have no idea why I let her get to me this morning. She does this so often I can usually just brush it off. For whatever reason, today it just hit me and here I am. A messy puddle in my own store." She sighed as she went to the counter to grab a tissue to dab at her eyes.

"Come on, I got Munch her frosted raspberry hand pie. Did you make the tea yet?"

"It's out back."

"Go sit at the counter. I'll go get the tea and some napkins. I'll be right back." Fee hurried to the back office. Her mind began to turn over Mrs. Johnson's parting words. Was it true? Did yelling at Mrs. Johnson that way make her a bad Christian? Could she have handled it another way?

Fiona knew as sure as she knew the sun would rise tomorrow that Mrs. Johnson would tell everyone about what had happened. What if it got back to Peter? What would he think? Would he agree with Mrs. Johnson and think how he had dodged a bullet by staying single? Should she have given more grace?

Sighing, she grabbed Kate's tea and started back to the front. It was too late now. Even if she were to chase Mrs. Johnson down and apologize, the woman wasn't known for her forgiving nature. Fiona would just have to wait to see.

"Lord, why did You have to give me red hair and the temper to match? Help me get this under control. Please. Make Your will known to me. If Peter is meant to be mine, please make that happen."

Fiona had come to terms with red hair when she was sixteen, but now? Now she wished deeply for blonde tresses with a mild temper. She snorted a laugh. It would seem the Lord still had many things yet for her to learn.

Chapter 17

♥

This was not going to end well. Peter stood on the edge of the ice arena watching people moving gracefully across the slick surface. He had grown up in Florida and didn't know how to ice skate. Yet here he was on a Saturday morning with a pair of hockey skates strapped to his feet.

"Hey mister, can I get by?"

"Oh sure, sorry about that." Peter carefully side stepped out of the way. A small boy launched himself onto the ice and immediately made off around the outer edge, leaning low, and pumping his arms for speed to catch up with friends at the other end. Peter stared as the trio of boys went whipping around the end without so much as a wobble.

Great. If he stepped foot on the ice, he would be shown up by young children. This was going to be a disaster.

He turned to head back to the benches to remove his skates. "Woah!"

Peter slammed into someone and felt himself wobbling. He blindly reached out, grabbing onto the arms of the person in front of him, holding on for dear life as he felt himself starting to fall.

"Lock your knees!"

Peter followed the command and found himself still upright, swaying a little, as he kept his grip on the person in front of him. He gave a sigh, "Thanks," and looked straight into the eyes of Fiona.

"Fee. You're here."

Peter couldn't believe how inane that sounded. Of course, she was here. He was holding on to her arms. Oh no, he was holding on to her. He quickly dropped his hands and tried to take a step back. He promptly started wobbling again.

"Hang on there, Peter. First time on skates?" He felt her grab ahold of him again.

Peter heard the amusement in Fiona's voice. "Yeah. How could you tell?" He laughed. "I was just going to go take them off. This is hopeless."

He saw Fiona raise one perfect eyebrow at him and give him a sassy grin. "Feeling a little cowardly today, Pastor?" The smile went full blown and his knees went a little weaker.

"Nothing wrong with preserving my tailbone."

"Worried what people might think?"

Fiona always had a way of hitting his soft spots. "I just don't want to fall and break something. I'm not as young as I used to be."

Fiona snorted with laughter, "Right, because you're ancient. Come on, I promise I won't let you fall."

"Fee..." but Peter's voice trailed off and he found himself walking gingerly after her, holding tight to her hand. He hadn't even realized he held her hand, but now he didn't want to let go.

"Okay, so stop walking like a robot. You need to loosen up."

"If I loosen up, I'm going to fall."

"No, if you *don't* loosen up, you *will* fall. Don't go all spaghetti arms and legs, but don't lock your knees, soften them just a little."

"Then why did you tell me to lock them a minute ago? I'm confused."

"Because you were on regular ground and looking to meet it head on. Now be quiet and follow my lead."

Fiona shot him a mischievous grin. He had a bad feeling about this, but he trusted Fiona. He was sure she wouldn't let anything happen. What could go wrong? Nothing more than breaking a wrist or a knee or his ego and pride. All were fixable. He hoped.

Fiona stopped just before stepping onto the ice and looked back over her shoulder at him. "We're going to step out on the ice and go right up against the glass on the other side."

Peter gripped the side of the opening with both hands as Fiona let go. She stepped smoothly onto the ice, spinning to face him, without a hitch or a bobble.

Peter's eyebrows rose. "I take it you know how to skate."

"I grew up in Maine, buddy. Of course, I know how to skate. I learned on the pond down the road from my house. And I skated with the boys." She lifted a foot to waggle the pink hockey skate attached. "No figure skates for me. Now stop stalling."

Peter wasn't sure what was happening right now, but he took a step forward and grabbed both of her hands. He held tight as he put one tentative foot on the ice.

"Don't look at your feet," Fiona directed him. "Look at me. Your feet know what to do. We just need to convince your mind of it."

Wasn't that the truth, he thought wryly. He looked up, eyes locked on Fiona's. *Gosh, she was so beautiful*. He forced himself to focus on where to put his feet. He placed his other foot forward and began to feel himself bobble.

"None of that now," Fiona said firmly. "Soften those knees and look at me."

Peter did as he was commanded, and the bobbling lessened.

"Okay, now stop thinking about how to walk. You don't walk on ice. You glide. I want you to push your right leg out to the side."

Peter again did as he was told and felt himself move forward slightly. Fiona still had hold of his hands and was moving backwards. Show off.

"Good! Now do the same with the left leg."

Again, Peter pushed his leg out and moved forward slightly.

"You're a natural, Peter."

"Don't placate me, Fiona. I'm only upright because you won't let me fall."

"You're right. I won't let you fall." She squeezed his hands and gave him a wink. "Now repeat what you just did."

The couple made their way awkwardly to the other end of the rink and around to the opposite side. Fiona coaxed Peter the whole way while he moved like a small child. He knew this to be true because there were kids in the center of the ring pushing around devices to help them stay upright. He liked having Fiona be his device, maybe a little too much.

"Let's take a break. Here, let me open the door. We can sit down for a minute."

Peter's ankles were burning from his efforts. He would be sore tomorrow. He sank gratefully onto the bench and put his legs out in front of him.

Fiona leaned against the short wall separating the ice from the benches. "Quite the turnout for the Community Cares kick off, don't you think?"

"It's amazing. All the local churches partnered with them. Last I heard, there were even enough mentors for all the kids."

"I can't wait to find out who I'm paired with. I have a lot of plans!" Fiona laughed and shifted her weight to her other leg.

"Why don't you go take a turn without me along as a handicap? I think I could use a little more time off skates."

"You sure? I don't mind helping you."

"I'm not sure I'll ever be a skater. I'm just hoping you'll bring me back to the exit so I can get off the ice without having to crawl."

Fiona laughed again. Peter loved making her laugh. She didn't hold back. It was loud and melodious.

"I won't make you do that, promise. Okay. I'll be back in a sec."

Fiona didn't even bother with the door. She hopped over the wall and took off, skating fast, crossing her feet as she came to the turn. She wove in and out of the people as if they were standing still. He saw her quickly come up to the other turn and whip around it, but this time she stayed facing backwards. It didn't seem to slow her down. She smiled and waved at him as she flew by for another lap.

Peter smiled. He loved how Fiona attacked life. She hadn't been bothered about helping him on the ice. And he knew she wasn't showing off now. She just knew how to enjoy what life brought her way. And right now, that was a pair of pink hockey skates and a rink of ice.

With a swish of skates, Fiona was back, stopping right in front of him. "Man, that was fun! Want me to take you around for a faster turn?"

"I'm sorry, what?"

"I can push you, and we can go a little faster if you want to try it. There's nothing like flying over the ice. I wish I could do this more often. I love skating."

"Fee, I don't think..."

Fiona gestured to him to stand up. "C'mon. It'll be fun. Trust me."

Peter was a goner once he saw the playful look in her eye. He couldn't resist. "Um, okay, but be gentle. I'm an old man."

Laughing, Fiona opened the door and held out a hand to him. "You're only three years older than me." She winked at him. "C'mon, old man. Let's have some fun."

Peter took a deep breath and stepped cautiously out on to the ice. Fiona skated behind him and placed her hands on his waist. Leaning forward, she spoke directly into his ear. "Just relax and trust me. Loosen your knees. Ready?"

Peter closed his eyes at the feel of her breath in his ear. It sent shivers down his spine. He opened them as he nodded. Fiona pushed off and they began to make their way around the rink. Fiona did go slower than she had alone, but it was much faster than Peter would have been able to do by himself.

Peter hoped the day wouldn't end anytime too soon.

Chapter 18

♥

F iona stifled another grin at seeing Peter wobble his way across the floor to take off his skates. He'd given her the perfect opportunity to connect when she saw him standing on shaky legs in the rink door.

She pushed off and took another few spins around the ice, forward and backward. People were beginning to head to the concessions area so the matches could be announced for the Community Cares program. Putting on a final burst of speed, she raced around the rink one last time, throwing up ice spray as she stopped.

She hurried to the changing area to unlace her skates and put on her boots. She was one of the last ones to enter the oversized concessions area. Scanning, she looked for an empty seat. Why hadn't she thought to ask Peter to save her one?

She spotted his brown head off to one side and started walking towards him. She could see there was an empty seat beside him. Smiling, she began to weave her way through the crowd still lingering and chatting near the door.

Just as she approached, a woman slipped into the seat beside Peter and gave him a smile. Stunned, Fiona stopped a few rows back. She watched as the two put their heads together to talk. Peter smiling at this…this…who was it?

Fuming, Fiona spun on her heel and walked to the other side of the room, plopping into an empty seat near the back corner. So, the man tells her he can't be in a relationship not more than a week ago and he's here with someone else? He never even mentioned anything when they were on the ice together. What kind of game was he playing?

Fiona craned her neck to see over the heads of those around her. She spotted Peter still sitting by the young blonde. The woman was pretty, Fiona would give her that. Fiona hadn't seen the other woman around town though. Who was she?

"Hey Fee, scooch over will ya?"

Fiona's turned to see Kate standing in the aisle. "I didn't know you were doing this, too. Don't you have enough going on right now?"

A voice came over the speakers at the front of the room. "Attention! Attention, please. Will everyone please find a seat? We will be making the matches shortly."

Kate sank into the chair beside Fiona. "I'm not doing it. I just wanted to meet your match. I figure I can act like an auntie." She raised an eyebrow at Fiona, "Have fun on the ice today?"

Fiona felt a blush rising but was stopped from replying as the Community Cares coordinator continued giving instructions. "Once matched, please go back to the table area to meet with your matches and their families. Use that time to plan out your schedule and get to know each other. Let's begin."

Fiona settled to wait for her name to be called. She couldn't help sneaking glances to where Peter was sitting. She could see him without making too much effort now that everyone else had finally settled into the chairs.

"Who are you looking at?" Kate leaned over to whisper to Fiona.

"No one. It's nothing."

"Right. Nothing. Like it's nothing that Peter's sitting with that other woman."

"Leave it alone, Kate."

"Do you know who it is?"

Fiona just shook her head and placed a finger against her own lips to signal Kate to be quiet. They were into the mentors with last names beginning with F. Her name should be called soon.

"It's Kelsey James."

Fiona gave her a quizzical look. "Who's that?"

"Peter's new secretary at the church."

The coordinator called out, "Fiona Gilliam and Sophie Roberts."

Fiona stood, ears still ringing with the words, "new secretary at church." Peter would be working with the woman daily. How was she supposed to compete with that?

Fiona walked to the front to meet the child she had been matched with. It was a young girl, about seven or eight years old, with light brown hair hanging in two braids to her shoulders. She had startling blue eyes with an adorable gap between her two front teeth.

"Hi, I'm Sophie! Are you Miss Fiona?"

Smiling and pushing thoughts of Peter behind her, Fiona held out her hand. "It's nice to meet you, Sophie. Let's go chat where it's quieter."

"Peter Grant and Brody Roberts."

Fiona heard Peter's name being called. She saw him stand and step around Kelsey. She worked on pushing the jealous feeling aside as she reached out to take Sophie's hand.

"That's my brother."

Fiona glanced down at the girl as a slightly older boy, maybe a year or two older than Sophie, walked to Peter and shook his hand.

"That boy is your brother?"

"Yup, Brody. Our mom is waiting over there for us. Let's go!"

Fiona followed the skipping little girl, refusing to glance behind her to see if Peter and Brody were following.

"Fiona! Wait up!"

Stopping, she turned to see Peter hurrying up with a smile on his face. "Looks like we're matched with a brother and sister. This is Brody."

"C'mon! I want some popcorn! I'm hungry!" Sophie called to the trio.

"She loves popcorn." Brody gave a shy smile and a shrug as he hurried towards his sister, leaving the two adults behind.

"Shall we?" Peter gestured forward with one arm for Fiona to lead.

Fiona smiled. She was hoping God wanted this relationship as much as she did, and maybe He did. Because she now had the perfect reason to contact Peter and to see him outside of church.

Blonde Kelsey didn't stand a chance.

Chapter 19

♥

It will be how long before you can get to it?" Peter let his head drop to his desk as he held the phone to his ear. A few water lines in the basement had frozen when the temperatures had dropped overnight. Peter hadn't realized the oil tanks were low and the heat had cut out right in the middle of the night when it was coldest.

Seaside Chapel was one of the oldest churches in Haven. First Baptist was located on the other side of town and St. Mary's was in the middle of town. Seaside had been built in the late 1800s, which meant many things had been updated or changed over the years.

When Seaside Chapel had been built, it hadn't had running water, bathrooms, or even electricity. The old gas light chandelier still hung in the middle of the sanctuary even though it was no longer used. The pews were original, polished with age and use, although the cushions on the seats were a new addition.

Other updates had been made including a larger stage area, lighting to make the worship team and pastor stand out a bit more, and the sound system was new last year. Paint and carpet had been added and updated over the years as well.

Peter hadn't known fully how much the other elders had done to make sure Seaside Chapel stayed in good shape. With the loss of Randy and Jesse from the elder board, things were beginning to fall by the wayside. Apparently, Jesse had overseen the building maintenance.

Peter knew he had a file here somewhere. He glanced around the piles of papers littering his desk. He didn't remember the last time oil had been delivered. Now he had a much bigger problem on his hands.

He needed oil today. He needed the lines thawed today. It looked like he was going to be on repair duty instead of working on his notes for Sunday. He was scheduled to go sledding later with Brody as well. He didn't want to cancel on their first outing.

"Okay, I get it, everyone needs you today, John."

"Sorry, Pastor. I'd love to help you but you're right. That cold snap last night really did a lot of damage. I'm heading out of town to work on a few homes with frozen pipes and it's going to take me all day. Philip is out sick so it's just me. I wish I could help."

"Thanks, John. I'll figure something out." Peter hung up the phone and stared at it. The oil company was sending a truck and a tech to get the furnace working, but it wouldn't matter if the lines were still frozen. It looked like the only plumber in town was busy.

Peter ran a hand through his hair in frustration. The women's auxiliary had started making noise about how things were not being done "like they used to be" since Randy and Jesse had left. They kept dropping hints, some not all that subtle, that Peter needed more help. He'd started finding slips of paper left on his desk with the names of various men in the church, and a few who weren't even members, for the open elder positions.

He would have to speak to the women soon. Right now, he needed to find someone who could help him get the lines thawed and fixed.

Grabbing his phone, he punched in the number for Drew. "Pick up. Pick up." The call went to voicemail. He felt the tension filling his body. He punched in Lucas's number next.

"Hey, what's up?"

"Any chance you can grab a blow torch and meet me at the church? Oh, and see if you can get any plumbing supplies from Drew while you're at it. He's not picking up."

"Did the lines freeze?"

"Yeah, and the oil truck is due this afternoon. I need to get the lines thawed and fixed ASAP. Any chance you can help me?"

"I'm off in about twenty minutes. Give me an hour to track down our brother and we'll meet you there."

Peter felt the relief surge through his body. "Thanks, man. I owe you one."

"You always do. See you in a few."

Peter hung up the phone and pulled his to do list closer. He reached over to crank up the electric heater he had going to keep the edge off the cold. The stone building held on to it tight.

He had thought hiring Kelsey would make things easier. It hadn't. Sure. The things that used to keep him busy were no longer the issue. However, now he had a whole new slew of items, like frozen water lines and empty oil tanks, taking him away from his sermon prep.

Peter leaned back in his chair and put his head back, closing his eyes. He felt the beginnings of a stress headache starting.

There was a knock on his door. "Come." Mrs. Johnson walked in, clutching her oversized purse in both hands. Peter contained his surprise. He couldn't remember a time Mrs. Johnson had *ever* knocked before entering.

His headache ramped up a notch. He knew Agnes Johnson was here to harp on her pet issue, the lack of deaconesses. She wanted the women of the church to have more of a leadership role. He'd been over this issue time and again with her. He wasn't up to the verbal sparring today.

"What can I help you with today, Mrs. Johnson?" *Please let it be easy. Please, Lord,* Peter thought as she took the chair across from him, settling her purse into her lap.

"I'm here on behalf of the women's auxiliary." She raised her nose, so she was looking down it at him. "And why is it so cold in here? Turn up the heat, young man!"

"I can't, Mrs. Johnson. The cold snap last night froze the pipes." Peter hated admitting that to her. He knew it would be one more black mark against him.

"Isn't there a brand-new furnace in the basement? I fail to understand how the lines are frozen if there is heat." She sat with arms crossed, a stern look on her face.

"We ran out of oil in the middle of the night. I'm waiting for a delivery and my brothers will be here soon to help thaw the lines. We'll have everything going again by this afternoon."

Mrs. Johnson sniffed. "This type of thing never happened when Jesse was in charge of building maintenance."

Peter sat silently. For once, she was right.

She continued, "I came here to discuss the women's auxiliary meeting we held last night. It's our opinion the leadership of the church is lacking. As such, we are calling for you to do one of three things and to do so immediately."

"I'm listening." Peter heard the implied "or else" in that statement. He wished he was anywhere but here. He knew God had called him into ministry, but it was times like this when he questioned why he stayed. He had a heart for people, he knew. But sometimes the extra grace required to deal with those who seemed to thrive on dissension made it hard to keep his focus on the overall point, which was to bring people to Christ and make disciples of them.

"There needs to be more accountability, Pastor. The women's auxiliary feels you need to appoint two more elders to replace Randy and Jesse. If you choose not to, then you need to allow the women's auxiliary to become deaconesses and take over some of those tasks."

"Mrs. Johnson, we've discussed this. I will not allow the women to become deaconesses. I've outlined this to you on numerous occasions."

"Then that leaves us with the third option."

Mrs. Johnson paused. She was going to be dramatic about it, which Peter disliked.

He urged her to continue, "Which is?"

"Your resignation. It's clear you have too much going on to lead effectively. If you won't find men to help you, then you need to leave your position. And after that public display with that redhead at the ice rink, it might be wise for you to do so. Good day."

Peter's mouth hung open as Mrs. Johnson marched from the room. Resign because the furnace ran out of oil? He had no doubt Mrs. Johnson had the ability to rally enough support to make it happen.

And what public display? He had skated with Fiona, if one could even call it that, nothing more.

"If you call that easy, Lord, we need to have a serious discussion." Peter put his now throbbing head down on the desk and began to pray earnestly for guidance.

Chapter 20

♥

F iona ran the duster over the shelves at Seascapes. Her mind kept wandering back to the Community Cares kick-off. She smiled as she thought about skating with Peter, which had been the highlight. It had been even better when they had been matched with siblings. It was like God was just giving her opportunities to hang out with Peter.

She was picking up Sophie after work today and going sledding at the big hill near the school. Haven Elementary School had been built at the top of a small rise. Every year a parent would take a snowmobile and run it up and down the hill, packing down a sledding track.

Fiona had tried to be subtle when she asked Leeann, Sophie's mom, if Brody was also going out. And from the sounds of it, Peter planned to take Brody sledding as well.

A smile covered her face as she dreamed about sharing a sled with Peter. She pulled out her phone to send him a quick text. *Sledding today? I'm picking up Sophie at 2pm if you want to meet us at the school.*

Just as she pocketed the phone, she heard the bell over the door tinkle. She looked up and froze in disbelief.

"Hey, beautiful."

Fiona could only stare as her ex-boyfriend, Henry North III, walked towards her.

He looked her up and down before pulling her in for a hug. He said, "You look fantastic. It's good to see you. It's been a while."

Fiona stood in shock, with her arms at her side. She came to her senses and pushed him away. She felt her temper rising but losing it twice in one week in the store wasn't good for business.

"What in blue blazes are you doing here?" She glanced around quickly, thankful there were no customers.

"I was passing through and wanted to pick up a gift for my mother."

Fiona snorted. "Lying has never looked good on you, Hank. What's the real reason?"

Henry, or Hank as he liked to be called to annoy his mother, was a smooth manipulator and a well accomplished liar. Fiona had learned that the hard way.

Once she thought herself in love enough with him to accept his proposal. She'd enjoyed the lifestyle he promised that came with fancy dinners and fancy houses, plural.

That was until she found him kissing the maid one day in the pantry, a very young maid. The problem was it happened soon after he had given Fiona a ring. He'd once promised everything to her before taking her heart and stomping all over it. He'd broken her trust. That was the day she'd packed her bags and left Boston to move back to Maine.

"Get out. I have nothing to say to you."

"Come on, honey. Give me a chance to explain."

"Save it for the next woman in line. I'm sure you have one or two in reserves. How many were there, Hank? How many before Rosie? One? Two? More?"

"Let's not rehash old details."

"Agreed. Now leave."

Fiona crossed her arms and glared at him. Her heart was still filled with contempt for not only the man in front of her but for the woman she'd been when she was with him. She'd made too many compromises along the way during their relationship instead of staying true to herself.

She thought she'd found the perfect man in Hank. She'd walked out of a local coffee shop on vacation one day while on the coast of Massachusetts and bumped into Hank. Literally bumped into him and almost spilled her coffee and his. They laughed and flirted. Before she knew it, she gave him her number and they started dating. Within ten months they were engaged.

Her first red flag that the relationship was doomed for failure should've been when she first met his parents. His mother had disapproved of her on sight. Agatha North did not like redheads. She even said that to Fiona's face. Agatha thought redheads were too passionate and too opinionated.

The ironic thing about it was Agatha was exactly those two things. Her husband had been more than willing to let her do and say whatever it was she wanted. He always meekly stood by and did as he was told. Fiona never once heard him tell his wife no.

"Fiona, I'm sorry. I was wrong."

She didn't even bother to hide her skepticism at those words, even if he looked like he meant them. She was sure he'd never said them to anyone before and certainly not to her.

"Hank, just leave. I'm not doing this again. It's over. Now go. There's nothing here for you. It's been over for more than a year. It's time for you to move on. I certainly have."

Hank's jaw clenched. He didn't like not getting what he wanted.

"What? Did you think I would be here just waiting for you?" Fiona laughed. "I've moved on, Hank. You need to as well."

"Let me show you I've changed." Hank reached out a hand to keep Fiona from turning away.

She raised an eyebrow at him. "Let me go. Now."

He pulled his hand away slowly. "Meet me for coffee. Just coffee. Let's talk. Can you give me that small courtesy?"

"That's rich. You ask me for courtesy when you couldn't even bring honor to our relationship."

"Hi! I'm Kate. And you are?"

Fiona spun to see her friend standing just outside the back room. Kate had gone out to make a deposit at the bank. Fiona was so focused on her confrontation with Hank, she hadn't heard Kate return.

Hank walked forward with his hand outstretched to shake Kate's. "Hank. Hank North. I'm an old friend of Fiona's. I was in town and wanted to see if she was available to catch up with me. I was hoping she could join me for coffee. I saw this bakery-diner-café place. Maybe you can help me convince her to take a break and sit with me for a little bit? I haven't seen her in ages."

Kate looked at Fiona with an eyebrow raised. Fiona raised one back and gave a slight shake of her head. Surely Kate would know what that meant.

"Fine with me." Kate gave a slight shrug of her shoulders.

It appeared Kate wasn't on the same wavelength. Fiona gave Kate a scowl before turning her full glare back on Hank.

"Fine. Coffee. That's it. I'll meet you there in fifteen minutes. Then you'll be leaving town, Hank. Agreed?"

"Let's talk before I agree to anything." He gave her a smile that once turned her knees to jelly. Now it simply made her want to smack his smug face.

Fiona sat in a booth at the Three Cats Café across from Hank wondering what she'd ever seen in him. The more he kept talking, the more she was convinced she must have been under the effect of some drug or magic or something. All Hank talked about since they'd received their coffee and pastries was himself. She'd yet to see any change in him.

"Father and Mother would love to see you again, Fiona."

She laughed. "Lying isn't going to make me change my mind, Hank. I haven't heard a lot of truth from you so far, but that was the biggest lie of all."

Hank's mother disliked that Fiona was "low class," as she called her. Fiona hadn't even known Hank's family was wealthy until they'd been dating for three months. At that point she'd been in love with him. He'd played her so well.

He'd taken her to his family's summer home on Nantucket. The "cottage" as he called it, had five bathrooms and ten bedrooms. The place was so enormous they even had staff to cook, clean, and maintain everything.

Hank and his family made their money from the hotel business. His great-great grandfather, George Abbot, started a small hotel. With good business practices over the years, the man had grown it into a successful chain of five-star hotels.

"I'm not lying. Mother said just the other day she missed the conversations she had with you. She really did like you. She just doesn't always show it. She's had too many people try to become friends with her when they find out she's an Abbot."

"Hank, your mother and I always argued. Those weren't conversations. She was constantly trying to get me to dye my hair black or brown or blonde, anything but red. She wanted to change the way I dressed or change the way I talked. Those were not exactly 'how are you, dear' conversations. C'mon, at least try to be truthful."

Fiona looked up as she heard the bell over the door. Peter walked in with Drew and Lucas. The brothers settled into a booth near the front. Peter hadn't seen her yet. She didn't know why she wanted him to. It wasn't like she wanted him to be jealous, but then again, a little jealousy sometimes worked.

Keeping an eye on Peter in her peripheral vision, she turned her head back to Hank. He was still going on about how much his family missed her, how much he missed her, and how much he'd changed. She could tell he was just saying what he thought she wanted to hear. The man really was clueless.

She saw the moment Peter realized she was sitting with another man. He started and stilled. She knew he was watching her. She took a deep breath and prayed for courage to make this work.

"Hank, listen."

Fiona reached across the table and placed her hand on his arm. She plastered a smile on her face in case Peter was still looking. She didn't dare glance over to check if she had his attention. She kept her focus on Hank instead.

"I think you believe you've changed, but you clearly haven't. All you've done today is talk about you and your family. Don't you care what I've been doing for the last year? Have you asked about me? No."

"But, Fiona, I was just trying to get you to see..." Hank placed his hand over hers where it lay on his arm.

Fiona yanked her hand away. "Stop it. You're not going to get your way this time. Let this go. Let me go. Leave Haven. This," she pointed to him and to her, "is not going to happen. It's just not. I've seen the real Henry North III and I don't like him. I liked Hank North, the charming guy who swept me off my feet one summer. The man who enjoyed spending time with me. Not the man who made promises he couldn't keep before we ever said, 'I do.'"

Leaning back, she removed her arm from under his hand. Hank's face hardened for a moment at the words before he forced a smile. There was something else going on here that

Fiona didn't understand. She wasn't interested in trying to figure it out either.

"Fiona, just give me another chance."

"Hi, Fiona. It's good to see you." Peter was standing beside the table. "Catch you at the sledding hill later?"

Shoot. Fiona had been so focused on Hank, she'd actually forgotten about Peter. He'd been able to sneak up on her. She wondered how much he'd overheard.

"Peter! Yes! The sledding hill. Later. Absolutely." She stopped talking. Anyone with ears would be able to hear how flustered she was. She saw Peter's eyes darken for a moment with something she couldn't quite identify as he glanced at Hank. She prayed she hadn't made a tactical error.

"Honey, aren't you going to introduce me?" Hank smoothly stood and held out his hand to shake Peter's. "Hello, I'm Hank North, Fiona's fiancée. And you are?"

Chapter 21

♥

Peter stood at the edge of the bluff watching as people careened down the sledding hill. He had his gloved hands pushed into his jacket pockets and shoulders hunched up by his ears trying to stay warm. Fiona had a fiancée. What kind of game was she playing and why did this bother him so much? God was his focus, not Fiona or any woman. Yet here he was, trying to figure out why he was so upset.

He knew he shouldn't be affected. Fiona was allowed to be with anyone she wanted. It just seemed his head and his heart couldn't get together on this issue. He was so sure God wanted him to stay single and live his life dedicated only to Him. And that was what he was trying to do. He'd pushed Fiona away and stuck her firmly in the friend-zone. Or so he thought until he came face to face with Hank North today.

"C'mon, Peter! Let's go!"

He raised a gloved hand at Brody and started towards him. "Coming!"

Peter tried to shake off thoughts of Fiona and Hank, but they'd followed him to the sledding hill. He felt the crack in his heart that started when the man introduced himself as Fiona's fiancé widening. Peter knew his focus hadn't been where it needed to be – on God. It had been on a woman, and it still was for that matter. A woman who had lied to him. A woman who had misled him. Foolish. So foolish.

He'd shaken the guy's hand like a robot. He didn't even remember anything that was said after that word, fiancée, was spoken. He pasted on a smile and left quickly to go pick up Brody. He knew he had to leave the café before he said or did something he would regret.

"Race you to the bottom!"

Brody jumped onto the plastic saucer sled and started spinning crazily down the hill. Laughing at the little boy's antics, Peter jumped on his own sled to give chase. Maybe what he needed was to let loose and enjoy being with Brody.

From what little Leeann had told him when he picked the boy up today, their father was out of the picture. They had no contact with him. She'd moved to Haven to get a fresh start. She would be starting at the church soon doing the cleaning and upkeep it so desperately needed, in addition to working part-time at the grocery store in town.

Peter landed beside Brody and watched the young boy leap to his feet.

"I beat you!"

"You sure did, kiddo."

"Wanna go again?"

"I think I'll watch you this time. Give me a chance to let these old bones rest a minute. Okay?"

"Sure! See you at the top!"

Brody run up the hill. Peter hadn't been lying. He was starting to feel a few bruises forming. He rose with a groan and started back up to the top. He hadn't thought thirty-two would feel this old, but it did today.

Laughter rang out. He worked on not turning his head but couldn't stop himself when he caught red hair flying down the hill. Fiona and Sophie were going down together on a longer plastic sled, both shrieking with laughter.

His eyes tracked them of their own accord, and he watched them slow at the bottom. Fiona dragged her feet to make the sled stop. He saw her hop out, grab the rope tied to the front, and pull the little girl back up the hill to go again.

"You look lost in thought."

Peter startled and turned to see Lucas walking toward him.

"Yeah. It's been a rough week. What are you doing here?"

"I saw your truck and thought I'd come see if it was true. I heard Pastor Peter was sledding and letting loose."

Peter let out a huff of laughter. "I like to have fun, you know."

"Yeah, but you rarely do. You're either at your new place working on something or at the church working on something else. So, what's up?"

"I'm here with Brody Roberts, my new Community Cares child."

"Is that the *only* reason you're here?" Lucas gave his brother a significant look as he nodded slightly towards where Fiona was readying to go down the hill with Sophie again.

Peter sighed. He hadn't told anyone about the problems at church, but this was Lucas. He could trust his brother, and he needed help processing everything. He was having such a hard time making decisions lately that he wasn't sure he could trust himself anymore.

"Fiona's engaged." Peter was surprised at the words coming out of his mouth. That wasn't the biggest issue he was facing, not by a long shot, with the ultimatum the women's auxiliary had given him.

"She's what? How can she be engaged? I didn't even know she was dating anyone."

"That makes two of us." Peter puffed out a breath of air. "I just met her fiancé. They were having lunch at Three Cats. His name is Hank North. Ever heard of him?"

"North. No, is he a local?"

"Didn't look like it. He had that polished city look about him." Peter turned to look out over the sledding hill again. "Nothing makes sense right now, Lucas. I don't know what to do."

Even that admission caused his chest to tighten. Peter always prided himself on being in control and knowing what the next right step was. He always felt he was following God fully and completely. He didn't like this feeling of being out of control. He certainly didn't like the feeling he'd had in the café when he saw Fiona touching another man's arm and smiling at him. He didn't like any of it.

"There's more." Peter swallowed hard. The words seemed to stick in his throat, "The church wants me to step down."

"What? Why?"

The look of alarm Lucas gave Peter caused more concern to bubble up in Peter's chest.

Waving his hand like it didn't matter, even though it did, Peter continued, "Mrs. Johnson is pushing for me to either add elders or make the women's auxiliary into a deaconess board. If I'm not willing to do one of those things, which is what I'm planning, she said the ladies will ask me to resign my position."

"Can they do that?"

"I'm sure they can make my life miserable, but they can't dismiss me out of hand. It would have to go before the elder board. If Tom and Will were to vote against me, it would be brought before the entire church membership, which would have to confirm their vote. So, yes, I suppose they could." Peter hoped he sounded believable. While he didn't think Tom and Will would vote against him, Mrs. Johnson could be very convincing when she wanted to be.

"Are you sure? You've seen Mrs. Johnson in action." Lucas gave an exaggerated shudder and smiled. "Do you want to go up against her and all the other women on the auxiliary? Wouldn't it be easier to find a couple men to add to the elder board? I know you don't want to leave Seaside."

"That's just it. I don't want to add anyone." The words shot out before Peter thought. He kept going. "The church is running smoothly." Peter stopped. That wasn't exactly true. "Well, it's running with a few potholes thrown in right now, but it'll work out. I just need to be patient, follow God, and make sure I'm following His will and no one else's. I don't think Mrs. Johnson is looking to do the same. She's always struck me as someone who wants to be in charge. If a deaconess board is formed, I bet I know who will lead it."

"Mrs. Johnson." The two brothers said the name together and grinned.

"I'll pray for you, brother." Lucas reached out and clasped Peter's shoulder. "What's going on with Fiona. I thought you declared yourself to be single for life. Rethinking that are we?" Lucas shot a smile at his brother and turned to watch the sledding action, giving Peter time to form a response.

"I thought that was what I wanted until I saw her with that guy. Something came alive inside of me. I haven't been in a fight since we were teenagers, but everything in me wanted to yank him out of that booth and punch him as hard as I could. Not exactly the thing a pastor should be doing." Peter gave Lucas a rueful look.

"Why do you think you felt that way?"

A laugh escaped as Peter watched children tumbling down the hill on sleds. "I'm not saying it."

"Chicken."

"Still not saying it."

"Coward." Lucas pushed a hand against Peter's shoulder.

"You can't make me say it."

"Wanna bet?" Lucas eyed his brother. "Let me give you some of Dad's advice. If you want to punch someone over a girl, it might be because you have more than friendship in mind with her."

Peter pushed his hands into his pockets, balling them into fists. His father always had pithy little statements of truth he would give the boys over the years. That one had come up more than once. It was always followed by "If you like the girl enough to punch someone over her, make sure you treat her with respect. Girls have feelings. Treat her like gold, and she'll treat you back the same way."

"I can't, Lucas. I just can't. I decided a few months ago to dedicate my life to building up the church and serving God. I can't go back on that now."

"Maybe you need to rethink your decision. Make sure it's what God wants of you and not just what you *think* God wants. We're not all called to be single. I know Paul himself stated that very thing. In fact, I'm pretty sure the words he used were 'But if they do not have self-control, let them marry; for it is better to marry than to burn with passion.' How did I do on that quote?"

"I'm not burning with passion."

"Really?" Lucas quirked one eyebrow at his brother. "What do you call this? You're standing up here, not having fun, I might add, brooding about a woman who is engaged to someone else. How exactly would you define 'burning with passion' if not that?"

"I'm not brooding. I'm thinking. There's a difference. And I can't have her so I'm not burning with anything." Peter hated the way he sounded right now and was having a hard time admitting Lucas might be right.

"Call it what you want."

Peter shook his head and watched as Brody went headfirst down the hill and landed in the snowbank at the bottom, feet sticking out, wiggling like mad. The young boy backed out, covered in snow, and laughing. Was Peter deluding himself over Fiona?

"I can't burn with passion for a woman who lied to me. She never told me she was dating or engaged."

"Why would she? You pushed her away, from what I heard. She had every right to find someone else. Someone who wanted her in their life. If you've changed your mind, you have two choices the way I see it."

"I don't want any more choices. I won't break up a relationship. Mrs. Johnson would have a field day with that one."

Lucas ignored his brother and continued. "Your first choice is to go tell Fiona how you feel. She's not married yet. There's time to make sure she's making the right decision."

The thought of telling Fiona how he felt tied his stomach in knots. It had been hard enough when they had been practicing the dance for Drew and Kate's wedding. He'd made a fool of himself time and time again, and she'd just laughed and reassured him. He'd loved spending time with her. It was during those lessons when he first felt himself thinking about her as more than a friend.

Peter shook off those thoughts. He didn't want to remember how he almost kissed her one day as he dipped her back at the end of the song. He'd seen a look in her eyes. One he wanted to explore at the time, but he'd stopped himself before making a mistake he couldn't fix. He needed to be an example to the community in how he presented himself with others, especially with single women. He couldn't just date to date. He had to date to marry.

Marry. Fiona was going to get married, and it wasn't going to be to him. His stomach dropped and Peter was pretty sure his heart stopped for a moment at realizing he could never have Fiona. Not if she was engaged to marry someone else.

"What's my second choice?"

"Your second choice, brother, is to walk away. Let her live her life as she's set it out and never bother her again. Can you live with that?"

Peter stilled and went cold at the realization he might never have Fiona. Never have Fee in his life? He wasn't sure he was ready for that. He grabbed the back of his neck. What was he going to do?

Lucas slapped a hand on Peter's shoulder. "Think about it, man. The choice will be simple when it's the right one."

Peter didn't even see his brother walk back to the parking lot, get in his car, and drive away. He stood on the hill, looking out at all the activity but seeing nothing. He had no idea what the next right step was and that scared him more than anything.

Chapter 22

♥

F iona stood near the checkout desk at Walden Memorial Library waiting for the story time to begin. She seemed to be on a roll lately, volunteering for new things. Today she was going to be reading to the six- to ten-year-olds.

Instead of looking at the book the librarian had given her, she was watching Sophie wander through the shelves of children's books.

"These are books anyone can read?" The child seemed mesmerized by the idea.

"Sure. If there's one you'd like to take home, I can help you set up a library card. We'll come every week if you want."

Sophie's eyes went round, and she turned back to the shelves with a look of determination on her face. "I need to find the best one!"

Fiona smiled as excitement fill the little girl's face. However, her mind was only on the fact she needed to clear things up with Peter. He'd left so quickly the other day she hadn't been able to clarify the situation.

As if she would ever agree to marry Hank. Her eyes were open now. There was only one man she could picture herself wanting to spend the rest of her life with, and it was not Henry North III.

She'd turned her fury on Hank as soon as Peter walked away. "What was that all about? We're not engaged anymore, Hank. I'm not your fiancée."

"You could be. Just say the word. I even have the ring right here." Hank pulled an engagement ring out of his pocket, placing it on the table in front of her.

"Put that away!" She'd hissed the words at him. "I'm not wearing it. We're not engaged!"

She'd stood and left knowing there was nothing else she could say. Hank never understood the word 'no'. She didn't know what Hank's plan was, but she knew there was more to it.

It seemed that instead of her actions causing Peter to see her as desirable, it had backfired. Operation Catch a Pastor was not going well at all.

"Hi, sweetie, I'm here. What do you want me to do?"

Fiona whirled. Hank was standing in front of her with an expectant look on his face.

"What are you doing here?" Fiona whispered the words at him, furious at the gall of the man to show up like this.

"I'm your helper. I signed up last week."

"Last week? You just showed up in town a few days ago." Fiona gave him an incredulous look. What *was* his game?

"I've been here for a couple of weeks. I wanted to give myself time to settle into Haven before I told you I was here."

"Why haven't I seen you around then? Haven isn't like Boston. It's hard for anyone new to go unnoticed for long. Have you been stalking me?" Fiona crossed her arms and scowled.

Bree had a stalker last year. Lucas had caught the man and put him in jail where he belonged. Fiona would do the same to Hank without missing a beat.

"I'm not stalking you. If I were, would I be here right now? I heard about this," he waved his hands around to take in the crowd of children growing around them, "and decided what better way to show you I've changed than to help out here."

"Right. Because you just love children?" Fiona didn't bother to try to hide the sarcasm.

That had been an issue between the two. Fiona wanted a large family. Hank wanted the requisite boy and girl. He used to make it sound like he could custom order his children like he custom ordered everything else.

Fiona had watched him with his niece and nephew one day when he didn't realize she was there. He'd ignored the two young children to the point where they were in danger of falling in the pool. The children were leaning over the side, trying to grab for a ball in the water, when Fiona raced to scoop them up before they fell in headfirst.

Hank hadn't understood why she was angry. "Hank! You were supposed to be keeping an eye on them. Not on your phone! What was so important you ignored them like that? They could have drowned!"

"You're overreacting, honey. See, they're fine."

The way he'd dismissed her concerns was upsetting. It was another red flag to why their relationship wouldn't have worked. He didn't care. There was no way he would do well with children. Not today. Not any day. He was too self-centered.

"Fiona, I do love children. That's why I'm here. I told you I've changed. Let me prove it."

"We'll see." Fiona couldn't tell him he couldn't help. After all, the entire program was being run by volunteers. It wasn't like she could pick and choose who helped. If she could, she certainly wouldn't have picked Hank.

The children's librarian approached the pair. "You can start anytime, Fiona. Just let me know if you need anything. Thanks for helping too, Hank."

It looked like Hank hadn't lied about signing up. Fiona shot him a glare and moved towards the rocking chair. Her mind was racing with a way to get rid of the man since he clearly wasn't leaving on his own.

"Hank, why don't you gather up the kids and sit with them. Maybe sit with some of the smaller ones to help them stay quiet and listen."

"Yeah, sure. I can do that."

Fiona watched as he stood doing nothing. He looked around the room as some of the boys played on the train table. Kids were darting in and out of the shelves and others were talking in the corners together. She wondered how long it would take him to get their attention and gather them up.

Fiona prodded him with a question, "Is there a problem?"

"What?" Hank jumped as if he'd forgotten where he was. "No, I've got it."

Fiona saw him start forward to a group of girls giggling in the corner. Their eyes went wide at his approach. Their chatter stopped abruptly, and they darted glances around looking for another adult. Hank shook his head and walked toward the boys at the train table. They didn't even look up at him when he spoke.

Fiona sighed. She tucked the book under her arm and clapped her hands together four times. Raising her voice, she said, "Hey kids! I've got this great story I'm going to read! It's got pirates and ships and battles and maybe even a princess. If you want to listen, come join me on the floor by the rocking chair."

She didn't even bother to hide the smile when the children stopped what they were doing and made their way to the rug near the chair.

Sophie sat front and center, a smile on her face, "Hurry Miss G! Hurry! I want to hear about the princess!"

Fiona saw Hank standing at the back of the room, as far from the kids as he could be and still be in the same room. It seemed some things never changed.

Chapter 23

♥

W e're going to see our baby! I can't wait." Kate squeezed her husband's hand as they walked into the hospital. There was some question about when the baby was due, so the doctor had ordered an ultrasound.

After checking in, they went to sit in the waiting area. Kate was nearly bouncing from the thought of seeing their baby on the screen. She knew she was pregnant. They'd had the test after all. The cravings she was having confirmed it, but there was something about seeing her baby today that felt almost surreal. It would show her this new little one she would be meeting in just a few months, and she was as excited as a child on Christmas morning.

It wasn't long before they were called back and settled into a room. Drew sat by Kate's head, holding her hand, while the tech started working. Kate watched as the tech moved the wand here and there, making some small comments about the head and the spine, pointing things out.

Kate's heart expanded with love as she met her child for the first time on the screen. She began to dream about who the baby would be like when it finally arrived. Would it be a little boy with blond hair and blue eyes like his daddy? Or would it be a little girl who looked like her? She prayed it would be a perfect combination of both.

Suddenly the tech went quiet and focused on the screen.

Kate felt dread flood her before she asked the tech, "Is everything okay?" She exchanged a worried glance with Drew. "What's wrong?"

"I'm just taking a few more measurements. I'll need to step out to speak with the doctor. Dr. Adams will be in shortly to see you."

Before Kate or Drew could ask anything else, the tech was gone.

With a look of horror, she stared at her husband. "Drew..."

"Don't worry, babe. Maybe this is routine. I've never done this before. Let's wait for Dr. Adams before we get too worked up."

She let Drew help her wipe the gel from her stomach and sit up on the side of the bed. Then she waited impatiently for Dr. Adams. She wanted reassurance everything was going to be okay.

To her untrained eyes, her baby had looked perfect. She was ecstatic to hear the heartbeat and see her little one moving around. She was just starting to feel butterfly flutters in her belly. The movement along with the ultrasound brought the reality home. She was going to have a baby, her own child. She pressed her hands harder against her stomach, praying everything was okay.

There was a knock on the door and Dr. Adams poked her head in. "Kate and Drew, will you follow me, please?"

"Is everything okay, Doc?" Kate heard the concern in her husband's voice as he asked the question.

"Please, let's talk in my office."

Kate felt a ball of dread form in her throat making it hard to swallow. She took Drew's hand and held on tight. Something was wrong, she knew it.

"Please, have a seat." Dr. Adams waved to the two chairs placed in front of her desk as she walked around to sit in her own chair. "I'm sorry. There's no easy way to say this. We found an issue with your baby on the ultrasound."

Kate felt tears begin to form. There couldn't be something wrong!

"It appears your daughter has a congenital heart issue. It looks like the main vessels from her heart are switched. The blood flow is compromised and will cause serious issues for her once she's born. She'll need surgery within the first week of life to fix the condition and it will be dangerous."

Kate felt the blood roaring in her ears. There was something wrong with her baby, her little girl! They had wanted to be surprised, but there was enough to deal with without being upset she now knew the baby's gender. Little Lori, named for her deceased sister. Her baby couldn't die like Lori!

"What are our options?" Drew asked.

Kate tried to focus on the question Drew had just asked. There had to be options. There were always options. There had to be one that would save their baby.

"This type of condition always requires surgery. It's called an arterial switch operation. It will need to happen within the first week. We'll likely transfer your daughter soon after birth to

Portland or even to Boston to have it done. I'll need to do some research on who to refer you to. The surgery should fix the issue, and she should do well after."

"That's a lot of 'shoulds' Dr. Adams," Drew said. "Are there any guarantees?"

"There aren't any guarantees with any surgery, I'm afraid. I'll start looking for the best surgeon to do this and get back to you soon. We found this early. Most people don't discover something's wrong until after the baby is born. We still have a few months to get everything set for the best possible outcome.

"Again, I'm so sorry. Keep doing all the things you're doing. You can't change it and worrying will make things harder for you. I'll talk to you soon."

"Doc, I'm afraid I have to disagree with you," Drew stated.

Kate looked at her husband. What did he disagree with?

"We serve a God who is the Great Physician. We're going to pray for this issue to be fixed before little Lori is even born. I trust my God to do it. Thanks." He stood and shook the doctor's hand, pulling Kate to her feet at the same time.

Now home, Kate sat on the couch, cuddled against her husband's side. She couldn't stop crying. The news about their little one's heart was still so shocking. She didn't understand how the Lord could bless them with a child and then have something so horribly wrong with her little heart.

"Shhhh...it's going to be okay, baby. God can heal our little one. Doctors don't always know everything." Drew reached down and touched her chin to bring her face up to look in his eyes. "He's still a God of miracles. We need to pray for one. And let others know so we can get them behind this, too. I really do believe God can heal our baby before she ever draws her first breath."

Kate took a deep breath. It felt like she'd done nothing but cry and try to breathe since their meeting with the doctor.

Kate had been shying away from even thinking the words, but she knew she needed to face it, and soon, if she wanted to move forward. Her baby, her precious little one being formed right now, had a congenital heart defect. She wondered yet again if it was because of something she had or hadn't done that caused it.

Drew gave her a gentle squeeze. "Stop. I can see you're thinking it. You didn't cause this. I didn't cause this. God didn't cause this. Sin in the world caused it. If you want to blame someone, blame Adam and Eve. It's their fault after all. If they had never eaten that apple, sin wouldn't have entered the world, and we would be living in perfect paradise right now."

She gave a hiccup that was halfway between a laugh and a cry. "I'll do that when I see them one day. Oh, Drew, what are we going to do?"

"We're going to pray. It's all we *can* do, and I know it's enough. Even if God doesn't heal our baby before she arrives, He can still heal her after. Either way, God's way is perfect. Do you believe that?"

"I want to. I so want to, but it's so hard. The thought of our little one having to have such major surgery after birth terrifies me." She stopped, placing her hands protectively over her abdomen.

Kate looked once more at her husband as he placed his large hand over both of hers and pressed. "Kate, I believe God is going to work a miracle. Pray with me. Let's pray over our little girl. God has her in His hands."

Tears dripped softly from Kate's eyes as she closed them and leaned into her husband, listening as his voice began to petition God for a miracle. Please God, do as he asks. Please give us this desire of our hearts. Please.

Chapter 24

♥

P eter picked up the stack of mail Kelsey had left for him. He flipped through to see what he might need to deal with before leaving to meet with Todd Danforth. Todd was a worship team leader. He'd called that morning asking to meet for coffee this afternoon. Peter prayed it wasn't more issues to add to his growing pile.

He was praying about the elders issue, but he hadn't felt like he had a good handle on who might fit the positions. He didn't want to be too hasty in his decision. He still wasn't convinced he needed to add anyone either. But with the women's auxiliary still threatening a coup, he knew he needed to do something.

Peter felt like he was struggling to find the perfect balance between sermon prep and the long list of other duties he had. Even with Kelsey taking over the administrative items, there was still so much more that went into making a church run smoothly. He felt behind and stressed at all the things he couldn't get to in a day. Too many distractions were still there.

Now he was also trying to fit in outings with Brody. The boy was a handful, but Peter sensed a deep need to connect with the boy. He wanted to do that for him. He saw his parents do that very thing with various kids over the years. He knew the benefits for not only the kids but for the adults as well. He just needed to figure out what to do with Brody this afternoon.

In the middle of the stack of mail, Peter saw an unmarked white envelope with his name written in block letters on the front. Curious, he opened it to find a single folded piece of paper with computer printed words centered on it all in caps.

I LIKE THE WAY YOU WATCH ME DURING THE SERVICE. I KNOW YOU FEEL SOMETHING TOO. I CAN TELL YOU WANT MORE. SO DO I.

What on earth? Who liked what? He stared down at the note. Walking quickly to the door, he opened it and poked his head out. "Hey Kelsey, got a minute?"

"Sure, what's up?"

"Do you know who dropped this off?" He handed her the note.

Kelsey's eyebrows raised as she read the words. "Woah. No, sorry, it was sitting on my desk this morning. I just put it in with the rest of the mail."

"Um, okay, thanks."

Peter went back into his office and closed the door. He needed to leave soon if he was going to meet Todd on time, but the note had him flustered.

Maybe Fiona had left it? Maybe she had snuck in after church on Sunday and dropped it on Kelsey's desk since his office was locked. No, that didn't make sense. Fiona was more straightforward than that.

He knew he hadn't singled anyone out during his sermon. He always kept his gaze moving throughout the congregation when he preached. He never let himself focus on one person too long. Well, except perhaps a certain redhead, and he even tried to avoid that lately or else he stumbled on his words.

Obviously, someone had gotten the wrong idea. The only person he liked was... He stopped the thought before it could form.

"Lord," he groaned to himself. "Help me. I thought you wanted me to stay focused on You and You alone, but I can't stop thinking about her."

Peter's head came up as he heard a knock on his door. "Come." Maybe Kelsey had remembered something after all.

Leeann poked her head through. "I just wanted to see if you needed anything else today. I'm just about finished."

"I'm heading out. I'll be out of your way in a minute."

"I already cleaned in here." She stepped through the door and gave him a large smile. "My kids are loving the Community Cares program. Thanks for all you're doing with Brody. He can't stop talking about you."

Peter smiled, "Thanks, he's a great kid. Is it still okay to swing by to get him after school? I thought we might go over to Ellsworth to the arcade for little bit."

"Yes, he'll love that. Well, I won't keep you. Have a great day."

After Leeann left, Peter tucked the note into the middle of his Bible. He thought it might be wise to keep it. His first impulse had been to toss it. He was sure it meant nothing, but maybe he should talk to Lucas about it first.

Grabbing his keys, he walked out to the hall. He didn't want to be late to meet Todd. He tapped lightly on Kelsey's open office door. "Hey, I'm headed out. I'll be back in about an hour or so."

"Sure thing. I'm going to take off a little early today if that's okay. I'm all caught up here."

"No problem. See you tomorrow."

Peter hoped Kelsey wouldn't mention anything. Maybe he should go back and tell her that. No, better to keep it low key and pretend as if it's nothing. He hoped it was nothing. He didn't need another complication right now. He had enough going on as it was.

An hour later, Peter sat behind the wheel of his truck with his head resting on the steering wheel. Todd had wanted to let him know he was stepping off the worship team. His shift at work had changed and he could no longer make rehearsals and even fewer services. This meant they would be short a keyboard player.

He laid his head back against his seat and closed his eyes. Maybe Mrs. Johnson and the women's auxiliary were right. Maybe he should resign. It was obvious as the days went by that he was not fit to lead Seaside Chapel. In the last few months everything that could go wrong, did. "What are you trying to teach me, Lord?"

Peter's head came up as his phone began to ring. He picked it up and saw his father's name on the screen. Punching the button, he answered. "Hey Dad."

"How are things going? I felt the need to check in on you. Everything okay?"

Peter sighed before he could catch himself. "Yeah. Everything's okay."

"That didn't sound convincing. Talk to me, son. What's going on?"

"It's such a mess up here, Dad." And before Peter could second guess himself, he laid out all his issues and concerns to his father. One thing Peter loved about his father was how well he listened. He didn't interrupt when someone was talking. He simply listened as Peter went over everything from the pipes freezing to Mrs. Johnson's ultimatum.

"So, it looks like I'll be resigning. I can't do it anymore, Dad. It's too much."

"You're right. You should resign."

Peter's mouth dropped open, and he pulled the phone away to stare at it. His father was siding with the women's auxiliary? He hadn't expected that. "I didn't think you'd take their side, Dad." He could feel anger rising. He always thought his father would see things his way.

"Peter, I am on your side, but you're trying to do too much. You're not following what God calls leaders to do. Think back to the story of Moses. Moses was doing what you are trying to do right now. He was trying to do it all. He was leading thousands of people through the wilderness. When you have that many people together there are bound to be issues, and he was one man trying to be the arbitrator of all of them."

"Well, I'm not trying to lead thousands here, Dad. I'm just trying to lead the few God has blessed me with."

"Be like Moses and listen to your elders." Peter heard the amusement in his father's voice as he continued, "Moses's very wise father-in-law, Jethro, looked at him one day and told him to find men he could trust to help with the burden. They would take care of the day-to-day things while Moses took care of the harder things. That would allow Moses to spend time with God, to hear from God, and to lead the people the way God intended him to.

"You need to find more elders. You need to get some trustworthy men to help you lead the church. You can't and you shouldn't be doing everything, Peter. If you continue with this path, you *should* resign. When you share the burden of leadership, it will become lighter."

"Thanks, Dad. I'll think about it. It's not going to be easy, though. I can't just snap my fingers and fix it."

"Don't complicate things. Just announce on Sunday how you're looking for some men who would be interested in serving. See who God brings forward. Trust Him, Peter. Trust Him and you won't go wrong."

"Thanks, Dad. I'm glad you called."

"Me too, son. Me too."

Hanging up, Peter put his truck in gear and made his way back to the church. He had an hour to wrap up his work there before he needed to go pick Brody up at his house. Maybe, just this once, he wouldn't worry about anything. He'd just pick up Brody and go have fun. He didn't want to think about the women's auxiliary or the elder board or even that strange note he'd found. Right now, he just wanted to forget everything.

"Trust, Lord. I get it. I need to trust You. And I do. Lead me in Your way, please." As Peter breathed the prayer, he pulled into the church parking lot. Looking up, he saw Fiona, leaning against her car staring right at him.

Chapter 25

♥

F iona watched as Peter parked his truck. She had a feeling
of déjà vu. She was here to confront him, just as she had
once before. Subtle was not one of her strong character traits.
She was done with him avoiding her.

She knew Peter was doing just that. It was a small town.
He was the pastor at the church she attended yet still was even
avoiding her there. It would have been obvious to anyone looking. Every time she tried to talk to him, he hurried in the opposite direction.

But every time she turned around, Hank seemed to be there.
She couldn't seem to get Hank to leave her be. And she was
getting very annoyed.

The church was locked when she'd arrived. She was just
about to get in her car to leave, when she saw Peter's truck
rounding the corner.

Fiona smiled a little as Peter stepped out of his truck and
walked towards her. There was no avoiding her now. "Hey."

"Hey yourself." She pushed herself off her car and walked towards him. He was dressed casually today in a pair of well-worn
jeans and a thick jacket. Today was warm for late January. With

the sun shining, it gave the illusion it was warmer than it really was.

He'd been running his hands through his hair again. He did that when he was thinking. She could tell from the furrows his fingers left behind. She tried to ignore the itch in her own fingers that wanted to follow the same paths.

He stopped in front of her and shuffled his feet. He kept his head down and didn't make eye contact. If she wasn't annoyed with him, she would think him adorable.

"I need to talk to you. Privately. Care to take a walk on the beach with me?" Fiona held her breath, unsure if he would agree or not. All she needed was for Mrs. Johnson to pop up and start scolding him about the impropriety of being alone with a single woman.

"Sure." He started in the direction of the shore front, and Fiona quickly caught up to walk beside him. She moved close, close enough that their hands brushed once as they walked. She felt him stiffen and shove his hands in his pockets.

So, it's like that is it? Well, we'll see about that, she thought. Peter was about to see just how stubborn Fiona could really be. The two made their way down the stone steps to the shore and started ambling along. Since she was on the beach, Fiona began to scan for pieces of sea glass as they walked.

"What did you want to talk about?" Peter kept his eyes straight ahead.

"Peter, look at me." Fiona stopped, turning to face him. She wanted to grab his arm but held back. After the last few times of having him reject her touch, she made herself wait.

Peter stopped but didn't look at her. "I can't do this, Fiona. I just can't. You're engaged. I..." He trailed off. She could tell he'd already said more than he wanted.

"First of all," she snapped, eyes blazing, "let's get one thing straight. I am *not* engaged."

Peter's head snapped up and he finally looked at her. "You're not. But he said..."

"You left before I could tell you otherwise and you've been avoiding me ever since. I am not engaged to Hank. No matter what he says."

"Then why would he say something like that?"

Fiona took a breath. This was the moment when things could go very wrong or very right. "We were engaged once. I broke it off over a year ago. The first time I saw him or talked to him since then was that day you saw us in the café."

"Oh."

Peter turned and continued down the beach. He raked his hand once more through his hair, grabbing the back of his neck.

Fiona followed but neither spoke until they were standing near the base of the lighthouse. They stood, facing the waves, watching them crash along the shoreline.

"Does he want you back?"

"He seems to think so, but I know better. The only thing Henry North III wants is himself. I caught him kissing one of the maids *after* we were engaged. I found out later there had been more than kissing and with more than just the maids. I count myself lucky I found out before the marriage."

"Then why is he here?" Fiona could see the confusion on Peter's face.

"I don't know, and I don't care. I'm telling you I'm not engaged. I'm telling you I don't want Hank North. I'm telling you..." Her eyes caught his and she hoped he could see everything there. Her anger drained, and she put her heart on display. Would he see it? She didn't want to be rejected again.

"Fee, there's something I need to tell you, too. I want..."

"Rocky! Come back!"

Fiona turned to see a large dog bearing down on them. "What is that?"

Fiona did not like big dogs, especially dogs that large galloping towards her. She took a quick step to stand behind Peter. She felt him put a hand back as if to protect her from the beast coming at them fast.

"I think it's a Great Dane. Or maybe it's a horse. It's hard to tell."

Fiona could hear a note of humor in Peter's voice.

"Don't let it eat me, whatever it is!"

"Don't worry, I'll protect you."

Fiona knew Peter was laughing at her, but she didn't care. That animal was huge!

"Rocky!"

Fiona felt Peter brace for impact. The dog didn't look like it was going to slow down.

"Rocky! Sit!"

At the last second, the large dog planted its feet, sliding to a stop, a foot away from where Peter and Fiona were standing. Fiona peeked over Peter's shoulder to see Kelsey running up to them.

Fiona felt like a gangly giant around the petite blonde. When Fiona had been young, she'd dreamed of having blonde hair, just like Kelsey's, with slight waves and not tight curls. It had taken her many years to come to terms with the fact that she would always be a curly redhead.

There wasn't much she could do about her height either. Fiona was five foot seven inches, which made her taller than the average woman but not too tall. Kelsey was at least two inches shorter, if not more. Fiona held back a sigh as the young woman arrived, slightly out of breath.

"Sorry about that. Rocky loves people, but always forgets how big she is." Turning to the dog, Kelsey gave her a stern look, "Rocky, stay."

The large beast sat in the sand, tongue lolling from its mouth in a happy doggy grin.

"Rocky? That's an unusual name for a girl," Peter said as he reached out a tentative hand to the dog. Rocky gave it a quick sniff before licking it. Peter laughed and began to rub the dog behind her ears.

With a loud doggy groan, Rocky dropped to the ground and rolled to her back, paws raised. "I see how it is. She's just looking for pets, isn't she? Aren't you? You big baby." Peter dropped to his knees beside the dog and began rubbing her belly.

Kelsey laughed. "You've figured her out on the first meeting. She's just an affection hound. Pathetic." Laughing again, Kelsey dropped to the sand beside Peter, and they both rubbed the pooch who groaned with doggy delight.

Fiona stood to the side, watching as Peter laughed with Kelsey. Kelsey, who worked with him all day long. Kelsey, who was younger and prettier. Kelsey, with the blonde hair and blue eyes. Kelsey, the perfect match for the bachelor minister at Seaside Chapel.

"I need to get back to the store. Nice seeing you, Kelsey. See you around, Peter." Fiona gave a sad smile to him as she turned to walk away. She thought there had been a moment when Peter was going to confess something to her. But the moment was gone, thanks to Rocky and Kelsey.

Chapter 26

♥

Peter glanced up as Fiona walked away. He had been about to ask her out on a date before Rocky and Kelsey interrupted them. He'd decided to let his foolish promise not to date go.

After his conversation with his father, he realized he wasn't trusting God. He was trusting in his own abilities. He was wrong about not adding elders to the church. He was also wrong about not pursuing the woman haunting his dreams.

He stood and started to follow Fiona. Kelsey laid a hand on his arm to stop him.

"Hang on, I wanted to let you know Leeann stopped by looking for you. She didn't say what she wanted, but I told her you had stepped out for a bit. I'm heading back as soon as I can pull Rocky here away from the beach. Poor thing hasn't gotten used to being inside all day. I adopted her just after I moved here. I like the company."

Peter's focus came back to the woman near him. He said, "I'm late picking up Brody. I need to get going. I'll touch base with Leeann. Thanks."

He looked once more to see how far Fiona had gotten and saw her just reaching the stairs that led to the parking lot. As she began to climb, Peter gave Rocky one last pat before standing. He brushed sand from his legs and shorts. "I'll see you later."

Kelsey finally released his arm. "Bye, Peter! See you tomorrow!"

With that, he broke into a jog towards the stairway. He could see Fiona almost to the top of the stairs. He quickened his pace to a run, arriving at the bottom, as Fiona disappeared at the top. "Fiona!" He called once and started up the stairs as fast as he could with shoes filled with cold sand.

Breathing hard, he reached the top but didn't see Fiona anywhere. "Fiona!" he called once more. Standing with sides heaving, hands on hips, he swiveled to look in every direction. She must have been moving faster than he thought.

He worked to catch his breath as he started walking fast back towards the church. Maybe he could catch Fiona before she got in her car and left. Seaside Chapel was only a block from the ocean.

Now that he'd resolved to not stay single, his one thought was how to convince Fiona he'd really changed his mind. He knew just how foolish it was to think he could forget Fiona. She'd embedded herself in his heart when they started dance lessons.

Peter stopped in his tracks. He really was such a fool. How could he have not known what he was feeling towards Fee? His thoughts in the morning were always about her. He noticed when she wasn't in church. He couldn't stop thinking about the Community Cares kick-off when she had taken him out on the ice. He had loved having her give him a skating lesson.

Arriving back at church, his heart sank as he saw Fiona's car was gone. She'd been faster than him. This time.

A smile crossed his face as he began to think what it might be like to go on a date with Fiona Gilliam. He couldn't wait to find out.

Peter needed to get the elders meeting going, but his mind was still focused on Fiona. He hadn't been able to connect with her since talking with her at the beach two days ago. She hadn't been at work or at home when he stopped by both places. He might have to enlist Kate's help for the next step. But he pushed the thoughts away. He needed to focus on this meeting.

Will and Tom sat across from him in his office. The older men were chatting about who they had seen that day. Peter had plans for this meeting tonight. Time to get going.

"Gentlemen, shall we pray and get started?" Without waiting for a response, Peter closed his eyes and prayed aloud for guidance and help for the meeting. He kept it short and to the point, but he made sure to mention adding new elders. He didn't want to take the men totally by surprise.

"Amen." The two men chorused as Peter closed the prayer and opened his eyes.

"You want to add more elders? Good. It's about time, young man." Will looked at Peter with a steely gaze. "I never did think we were enough to lead this church."

Peter kept his jaw in place even though he wanted to let it fall open in shock. Maybe Will and Tom weren't as oblivious as he'd thought. He cleared his throat. "Yes, I have some candidates in mind. Since the two of you have been members of this church and community far longer than I have, I want to know what you think of each one."

"Sure, sure. Who did you have in mind?" Will seemed to be the spokesman tonight. Tom was the quieter of the two. He was a deep thinker and only spoke when he knew he had something to contribute.

"Alan Columbus."

Before Peter could go any further, Will interrupted him. "No, no. No good. Alan can never commit to anything. He'll say he can do it, and I think he means it, but he never follows through. Right, Tom?"

Tom simply nodded his agreement.

Peter scratched the name off the list, moving on to the next. "Joshua Silverstein."

"He's new around here. I think he moved to Haven ten years ago."

Peter stifled a grin. Ten years in town, and Joshua was still considered "new." He supposed if one had been born here and was pushing ninety years old, that would indeed be new.

Will continued with his assessment of Joshua. "I can't think of anything that might disqualify him. Seems like a nice enough guy. His wife is lovely. She brought me some chicken soup once when I was sick. You could put his name on your list there."

Tom once more nodded in agreement.

"Albert Cunningham."

"Nope." Will crossed his arms and sat back.

"No? Why not?" Peter had never seen Will put his foot down on anything this quickly.

"He's a liar and a cheat."

"Care to elaborate on that? He is a member here."

"He promised me a gallon of maple syrup a few years back. He never got it to me. When I asked him about it, he denied it. I had to buy my own gallon that year and it's expensive stuff! He never should have offered it if he wasn't going to follow through."

Peter crossed off the name. He was sure there was more to the story than Will's side, but he needed all the elders to work together. He couldn't ask someone to join if Will, or Tom for that matter, had issues between them. However, he thought he might need to address the issue of forgiveness soon. Again.

"Well, that just leaves one more name. I'd really like to have a full board again so if Joshua is amenable, we'll add him."

Peter glanced at the last name on his list. He took a deep breath before looking up. He prayed the men would see this as a good thing.

"The last name on my list is Drew Grant."

Peter paused and waited. Will didn't speak immediately. Would the other two men think he was trying to stack the board by adding his brother? He'd prayed about this long and hard before adding Drew's name.

These two old-timers would consider Drew "new." Peter hoped they wouldn't count it against his brother. Drew always lent a hand when repairs were needed and worked as a de facto handyman for the church. He was also a member of the worship team, often leading worship on Sunday mornings.

Will continued as the spokesman, "I think we both agree Drew would be a good fit. Looks like we have two names. Now what Pastor?"

Peter's head shot up. He needed to stay focused. Placing a check mark beside Drew's name, he smiled at the two men across from him. "Thank you, gentlemen. I'll have lunch with them both in the next week. Then hopefully we can work on getting them installed on the board."

As the older men began chatting about the best fishing spots, Peter smiled. For the first time in a long time, he felt hope and peace fill him. Hope he wasn't going to ruin Seaside Chapel, and peace he was finally following God's will.

Chapter 27

♥

People watching from her favorite booth at the Three Cat Café, was one of Fiona's favorite things to do. It also meant she didn't have to figure out what to cook for herself. She really disliked cooking. The burnt toast in her trash proved how bad she was at it. How pathetic was that?

She scrolled through social media as she waited for her meal to arrive. Sipping mindlessly on her coffee, she sat up, startled at what she was seeing. Using her thumb to back up, she stared at a photo of Peter. She sat her coffee cup on the table as she raised her phone closer, squinting. She had to be seeing things.

She read the words posted with the photo. *What a great day! I'm pretty sure Rocky is smitten with Peter!* Kelsey. She sat her phone down, closing her eyes. Maybe if she took a minute, she would open them and see something different. She huffed out a breath and picked her phone back up.

No such luck. The photo was still there. It showed Peter kneeling on the beach, rubbing a dog's belly. Rocky's head was to the side, tongue hanging out of her mouth in an upside-down doggie grin.

Fiona sat back against the booth, stunned. She wanted to think Peter was interested in her, but was he really? Fiona tried to recall if she was even friends with Kelsey online. Checking, she realized she was seeing the post because Kelsey had tagged Peter in it.

Noticing there were comments on the picture, she tapped to open them. The blood drained from her face as she read.

He's gorgeous! Way to go, Kelsey!

Hubba, hubba! I'd go to his church anytime. What a hottie!

You got a dog!!! No way! And who's the cute guy with you? What's his name? And the dog's cute too!

How long have you been dating that guy? Gorgeous!

"Here you go, sweetie. Anything else?"

Fiona jumped as the plate of food slid into place in front of her. She looked up to see Bree standing next to her, waiting for an answer.

She shook her head, trying to hide how flustered she was. "I'm sorry, what? Oh, no. I'm good. Thanks."

"Are you okay, Fee?" Bree slid onto the bench across from her. "You don't look good."

"Here." She slid her phone across to Bree. "What do you make of that?"

Fiona wasn't sure she could trust her feelings. After all, she didn't even have a relationship beyond friendship with Peter. Why should it matter if Kelsey had posted a photo of him with her dog? But it did. It did because to her eyes it looked like they were in a relationship. And Peter had specifically told her he wasn't interested in a relationship with anyone. Maybe he meant just Fiona. She worked on keeping her emotions from running ahead of the truth.

As Bree took her phone, Fiona said, "Make sure to read the comments, too."

The smile that covered Bree's face at the sight of the photo began to fade as she read.

Without a word, Bree slid the phone back to Fiona.

Fiona held her breath and waited. She was praying she'd taken it out of context. "Well?"

"When did they start dating?" Bree gave Fiona a look of confusion.

Fiona's heart sunk. "I don't know. I was standing just outside that photo, Bree. Peter and I were walking on the beach when her dog came running up and interrupted us. He was just about to tell me something. I think it was important. But now there's this." She pointed at her phone.

Bree reached over and squeezed Fiona's hand. "Fee, you need to tell that man how you feel and soon."

"I did – that day! Just before Kelsey showed up. But what if they *are* dating? I don't want to come between anything. I shouldn't do that. Right?"

"You need all the facts. Ask Kate. She'll know if Peter's dating anyone. He'll have told Drew. Call her. I need to get back to work but call her. And I'll ask Lucas when I see him next. We'll get to the bottom of it, I promise. You and Peter are made for each other." She winked at Fiona, "You just need to get out of each other's way."

Standing up, Bree reached out a hand and squeezed Fiona's shoulder. She gave her one more bit of encouragement before leaving, "It'll be okay. Remember, God's will above all else."

Fiona looked at the photo again. Maybe she was reading too much into this. Peter looked so relaxed. More relaxed than she had ever seen him. She just wished she knew what he'd been about to say.

"Hi beautiful. Care if I join you?"

Fiona startled again as Hank slid into the booth across from her. Her mood darkened at the sight of him. What was his purpose for being in Haven? He kept telling her it was to win her back, but she didn't believe it for one second. Hank's only goal in life was to satisfy himself. If he was here, there had to be another reason.

Fiona had been appalled near the end of their relationship as Hank took whatever he desired. She wouldn't be another thing he could check off as having won. The man needed to realize he couldn't always get his own way.

Was that why he was here? She'd left him, not the other way around. In fact, Hank had tried to convince her she hadn't seen what she knew was true. He'd tried more than once to convince her to come back to him before she moved to Haven. It was clear it wasn't because he loved her. He only wanted her to stand on his arm and look pretty. Nothing more.

"What do you want, Hank? I'm busy. Go away." Being direct was the only way to deal with Henry North III. She crossed her arms and sat back, shooting him a glare.

"Now, now, sweetie. I just wanted to see how you were doing. I've missed you. I told you that." Hank raised a hand and signaled Bree.

Fiona saw the look of distaste on Bree's face as she glanced at Hank before she quickly wiped it off, ever the professional. She had, what Fiona called, her "waitress face" on by the time she arrived at the table.

"I'll have a cup of coffee, black. And a plate of eggs, over easy, with a side of bacon. And add a blueberry scone too while you're at it."

Fiona waited, but Hank simply turned and looked at her with a smile that didn't quite reach his eyes. Sighing, she turned to call after Bree, "Thank you!" She gave Hank a raised eyebrow.

"What?"

He had a look of such innocence on his face. Fiona felt her anger rising at all men. Hank was so clueless. In his world, people waited on him. It was just expected.

"Nothing." She shook her head and began to eat her food. "Please leave."

"Now, that's no way to talk to me. I'm not leaving until you agree to go out with me. You know you miss me."

Hank placed his hands on the table and leaned forward. Fiona realized he thought she was playing hard to catch. Hank always did the rejecting.

"I'm not interested, Hank. Now leave so I can finish my breakfast in peace."

She put her head down and continued eating. Maybe he'd leave if she ignored him. Doubtful, but she could hope.

Looking up as the bell on the door gave a ding, she saw Peter and Kelsey walk in together, laughing. The bite of egg she'd just put in her mouth lodged in her throat. She grabbed for her orange juice, taking a large swallow to try to dislodge the food. Peter was here with Kelsey, and Fiona knew it wasn't Kelsey's day to work. Why would Peter be spending time with her outside of church if they weren't dating?

Swallowing hard, Fiona looked at Hank again. "Fine. I'll go out with you. Pick me up at seven on Friday. I'll text you my address."

Standing abruptly, Fiona shot out, "And you can pay for my breakfast as a sign of goodwill." Turning on her heel, she walked past the counter where Peter and Kelsey were now seated. Peter never even saw her leave.

If Peter had moved on, then so would she. Even so, she was already regretting telling Hank yes.

Chapter 28

♥

P eter hummed along to the radio as he pulled into the church on Thursday night. He was looking forward to practice for the worship team. It had been far too long since he had played the piano. He hoped he was up to the task. The last thing he wanted was to be on stage with the team and let them down.

He walked to the side door, pulling it open. He wanted to stop by his office first to grab his sermon notes so he could go over it again tonight once he was home. He thought he could weave in the lyrics to some of the songs they would be using to tie everything together.

Flipping on the light switch, Peter walked swiftly to his desk and grabbed the notes. As he turned, something fell to the floor. A plain white envelope lay by his foot. He leaned over and picked it up.

His name was written in block letters on the front, just like the other note. His insides clenched. Lifting the flap, he pulled out the notecard inside.

YOU CAN'T HIDE IT. I KNOW YOU LIKE ME TOO.

While he'd tried to push off the first note as nothing, he now wondered if that was a good idea. Was he giving off a vibe to someone in the church and didn't realize it? Why else would someone leave a note like this for him? And why didn't they want him to know who they were? He racked his mind for anything he might have done that could have been taken the wrong way.

"Hey, are you joining us? We're just about ready to start."

Peter looked up as Drew walked into the office. "What? Oh, yeah. I was just grabbing something."

"What's that?" Drew pointed at the card in Peter's hand.

"Take a look, and you tell me." Peter handed the card to his brother and watched as he read it.

"No signature, huh? That's weird."

"That's what I thought, and it's not the first one." Peter walked around his desk and picked up his Bible. He flipped it open and took out the other note. "Here."

Who had access to his office? Who knew when he would be gone so they could slip them in? Based on the first note, it had to be someone who came to church.

Drew handed the notes back to Peter. Instead of tucking them in his Bible this time, he placed them in his top desk drawer and locked it.

"What do you think?" Peter asked his brother.

"Well, someone thinks highly of you, but quite frankly it's a little creepy. Why don't they just come out and say it to your face instead of leaving you these notes to find?"

Peter rubbed a hand through his hair. He knew who he *wanted* it to be, but she'd just told him in person what she thought of him. It didn't make sense she'd leave him notes. He was so confused.

"What about your new secretary?" Drew asked.

"Kelsey?" Peter looked incredulously at his brother. "I don't think so. I don't think she'd leave me notes like that. I'm too old for her anyway."

"But that might be exactly why it could be her. Maybe she doesn't want to come right out and tell you because she likes the job, and she's afraid you'll fire her. Maybe she's waiting for you to figure it out and ask her on a date."

Peter was already shaking his head. "No, I can't see it. She treats me professionally. I don't get that vibe from her."

"Really? What do you make of this?" Drew took his phone out of his pocket and held up a finger. "Give me a second to find it."

Peter waited for his brother as he continued to go through the possibilities. He kept landing on the hope it was Fiona. If it were her, it would be rather sweet.

"Here." Drew pushed his phone at him. "Kelsey posted that a couple days ago. I've been meaning to ask you about it."

Peter looked at the photo of himself playing with Kelsey's dog on the beach. He saw the tag on the post, but he hadn't been on social media in days. He often wasn't. He didn't even know why he'd ever set up a profile.

It had been an innocent meeting. Fiona had been right there. Nowhere was it obvious Fiona was standing outside the camera shot. The caption made it seem as if Peter had been on the beach with Kelsey and her dog. His stomach sank when he realized not only had it been posted publicly but he'd been tagged. He swallowed hard. What were people saying?

"It's not what it looks like." Peter handed his brother back his phone.

"It looks like the two of you were on a date. Did you see the comments? Someone even asked her how long you've been dating."

"What did she say?"

"She hasn't answered it."

"We weren't on a date, and we aren't dating. In fact, Fiona was standing just out of camera range. I don't even remember Kelsey taking a photo. Fiona and I were walking on the beach together just before when Rocky came up to us. In fact, I was..." Peter let his voice trail off.

"You were what?"

"It doesn't matter."

"Something is going on here, bro. Something that could cause you some trouble. You might want to let me know what it is so I can help you."

Peter looked at Drew. He was right. "I was going to ask Fiona out on a date."

Drew's eyebrows went up. "I thought you'd sworn off women, including Fiona. What happened to all that?"

"I know. That was before I talked to Dad."

Drew grinned. "Really?"

Peter eyed him. "Did you call him?"

"I plead the fifth." Drew's grin widened. "So, dating Fiona, are we?"

"I'm not dating anyone. Before I could ask Fiona out, Kelsey's dog came running up. She interrupted us, and I never got a chance to ask Fiona. Fee left and I ran after her, but she moved too fast. I haven't seen her since."

"Well, she saw you."

"What? When? Where?"

"Slow down. She saw you and Kelsey in the Three Cats laughing together. She was sitting in her corner booth with Hank. And she agreed to go out with him tomorrow night. Bree and Kate were talking when I went to bring Kate a hot chocolate and cinnamon bun that Munch apparently *needed* this afternoon."

Peter raked his fingers through his hair once again, groaning. "What am I going to do now?"

"First, you're going to come with me so we can get this rehearsal going. Second, you're going to call Fiona tonight and set things straight. Ask the woman out. And we can double date if that's easier. Just do it. Kate will be over the moon about all this. And you didn't hear this from me, but someone else, until yesterday at least, was also eager to go on a date with you."

Drew clapped a hand on Peter's shoulder. "Stop worrying, Peter. There's nothing you can do right now. So, let's go make music to the Lord."

Peter's heart leapt in his chest at Drew's words of Fiona being eager to date him. He prayed he could make this all right with Fiona. Now that he knew what he wanted, he was eager to move forward.

Chapter 29

♥

F iona held back a sigh. It was her birthday, and she was all alone. Again. She used to think she would be married by the time she was this age. Except, here she was knocking on the door of thirty, and still single. No children. No house. No cute, fluffy dog to cuddle.

Sighing, she pushed the thoughts to the back of her head as she pulled open the door of the Three Cats Café. She'd poured out her heart to Kate just the other day after seeing the post with Peter and Kelsey's dog. The hurt from him giving up his no dating rule to date Kelsey was still poking at her heart. Operation Catch a Pastor had crashed and burned.

Slipping onto a stool at the counter, Fiona felt tears filling her eyes, but she refused to let them spill over. She squared her shoulders. She'd promised herself to never cry over another man and she wasn't going to start now.

Kate had assured her that Peter wasn't dating Kelsey, but Fiona knew what she'd seen. Peter flirting, laughing, and dining with the woman. It was the very definition of dating.

"What can I get you, honey?"

Fiona looked up at Brenda Stone. Brenda was Fiona's favorite sister of the three who owned the café. She was also the mastermind behind all the scrumptious baked goods in the cabinet near the cash register. "Can I get a frosted raspberry hand pie and a frosted cherry hand pie to go?" She hadn't meant to order two pies, but now that she had, she decided to let the order stand. "And I'll take a large coffee with three creams, too. Thanks."

Since Kate had been on a hand pie kick, Fiona bought one for her friend every time she came in. Fiona's jeans were telling her she needed to be more careful, but since it was her birthday, she was going all in.

She wasn't going to feel sorry for herself. She just wasn't. What was it Kate had said just the other day? God knows us. He knows our deepest desire. He has a way of turning bad things into good.

"Here you go. Everything okay, dear?" Brenda handed across the coffee cup and the pastry bag.

Fiona snapped out of her musings. Smiling, she laid the cash on the counter and picked up her food and drink. "I'm good, Brenda. Thanks." Maybe she just needed to change her mindset. Instead of focusing on what she didn't have, she'd look at what she did have.

With the coffee and pastry bag in hand, Fiona left. Her heart wanted Peter, but things weren't working out that way. In fact, Fiona was going on that date with Hank tonight.

She doubted Hank would remember it was her birthday. He never had when they were together. She didn't expect he would now either.

Part of her wanted to cancel tonight. The other part wanted to confront Hank once more over his reasons for being here. She knew there was more to his coming to Haven than he was letting on. She just hoped she wouldn't regret agreeing to tonight.

Kate had given her today off from the store because of her birthday. Normally, they would have gone out to eat, but Fiona had told her about the date with Hank. Kate hadn't been keen on Fiona going out with him that night. She'd told her, "You should spend it with someone who cares about you."

Fiona knew her friend was just trying to help. But now that Peter was with Kelsey, Fiona would have to get used to that. Her stomach clenched at the thought, and she wasn't sure she'd be able to eat any of her hand pies.

She picked her way over the boulders along the shoreline and found a flat one to sit on. She was bundled in her jacket and was thankful the sun was out. She lifted her face to gather the warmth. February was such a hit or miss time in Maine for weather. Today was a good day, but she remembered birthdays with ice covered trees outside and snow piled up.

Setting the bag and coffee beside her, she pulled her knees into her chest. Laying her head on her folded arms on top of her knees, she closed her eyes and prayed silently.

Lord, I want what You have planned for my life. I want a man who loves me like You do. I want a man who desires to follow You with everything he has in him. Heal my heart. Make it open to what Your will is for me.

"Mind if I join you?"

Fiona started and opened her eyes. Peter was standing on the shore in front of her, hands in his jacket pockets, looking far more adorable than he had a right to. *Lord, why do you continue to taunt me like this?*

"Sure." She didn't know what made her answer in the affirmative. Except there was no getting around the fact that Fiona's best friend was married to Peter's brother. They would see each other often. She needed to figure out how to be friends with him.

Peter made his way across the boulders and sat beside her, just out of reach. Pulling the pastry bag close, she took out the cherry one. Handing the bag to Peter, she asked, "Want it?"

"Thanks," Peter said as he reached in, pulling the pastry out and taking a bite. His eyes closed as he gave out a small groan.

Fiona felt her stomach leap at the sound. *Pull it together, Fee.*

Peter mumbled around the bite in his mouth, "Raspberry is my favorite."

She smiled and prayed the Lord would hold back the blush she could feel building. *Friends, Fee, just friends.*

The two chewed quietly beside each other, enjoying the late afternoon sun. Fiona always felt like her birthday signaled the end of winter. Spring would be here soon.

"I hear it's your birthday."

Fiona's head whipped to the side. She hadn't told him that. Kate. Kate must have said something. Was her friend interfering in her life? Did she *want* her friend interfering? If she was honest, maybe. Maybe she did.

Turning back to the view of the waves, she casually answered, "It is." She took a sip of coffee. She could be quiet. She wasn't always an extroverted-life-of-the-party person. She could be reserved with effort when needed. And right now, she was just tired. She was tired of trying to figure out what this man next to her was doing.

"I was wondering..."

Fiona turned to look at Peter as his words trailed off. "Wondering what?"

Peter cleared his throat and... was he blushing? Fiona took another sip of coffee and worked to hide a smile. She was enjoying this discombobulated Peter. It was hard to be mad at him.

"I was wondering if you'd like to go to dinner with me tonight. To celebrate your birthday."

Fiona raised an eyebrow at him as her anger once more started to build. "Don't you think dating one woman is enough?"

She stood, working to keep her anger controlled. She gathered her trash in one hand. She'd wanted Peter to ask her out for so long, and now that he had, she was mad. Mad that he thought he could date more than one woman at a time.

"Wait!" Peter reached out to grab her arm as she started to step to the boulder above them.

Fiona glanced from her arm to his eyes, and he released it. Peter swallowed hard before continuing, "Please, let me explain. I *do* think dating one woman is enough. I was hoping that woman would be you."

Fiona couldn't help herself, she snorted. "I'm not good at sharing." She started climbing back to the parking lot.

"Fiona!"

"I don't have time for your games, Peter," she called over her shoulder.

Peter reached out and grabbed her arm again, pulling her back around to face him just as she reached the lot. "I'm doing this all wrong. Just listen to me. I'm not dating Kelsey."

Fiona pulled her arm free and turned her back to him. Could she trust him? Hank used to tell her there was no one else until she'd caught him red-handed.

"Fiona, please. I'm not dating Kelsey. I wouldn't lie to you."

Slowly turning, she met Peter's eyes and saw the sincerity in them. "Does she know that?"

"I have no idea. Even if she doesn't, it's still true."

Kate told her God would grant her the desires of her heart if Fiona believed. She only needed to trust in Him for His timing and not hers. Taking a deep breath, she realized it was time to see if that was true.

"Fine. I'll go out with you, but if you're lying to me Peter Grant, I will make sure you regret it."

A smile lit up his face. "You won't regret it, Fee. I promise. I'll pick you up at seven."

Chapter 30

♥

P eter whistled softly to himself as he snatched up his keys and hurried out the door. He was running late to pick up Fiona. He smiled as he jumped into his truck and started across town to her apartment. He was going to take her out to eat at the new restaurant, Haven Light. It was located near the lighthouse, and everyone was raving about it.

He shook his head at the turn of events. Here he was, an introverted pastor who didn't really like the spotlight, taking out one of the most extroverted people he'd ever met.

Peter certainly enjoyed teaching and preaching on Sundays. He felt God had called him to the pulpit after all. He just enjoyed more intimate gatherings with fewer people. Not exactly a great thing for a pastor. He often had to push himself out of his comfort zone.

Fiona, however, was larger than life. Her exuberance was one thing that drew Peter. It had from the very beginning. Her smile which always lit up a room. She always seemed to enjoy life and everything it had to offer. Peter was eager to see what life looked like through her eyes.

He found himself pushing the gas pedal a little harder. He couldn't wait to see her. Now that he'd decided he was going to pursue Fiona, he was having to pull himself back some. He needed to give Fiona time to get used to the idea he was in her life for good.

Blue lights flashed in his rearview mirror. He groaned. Seriously?

He flipped on a blinker and pulled to the side of the road. If this was Lucas, he was going to...

"Evening, license, registration, and insurance please, Peter."

Looking up, Peter saw the wide grin of his brother looking down at him. "Lucas, I don't have time for this. I'm late."

"Need to set a good example for the folks of Haven, don't we? I clocked you going almost ten miles over. License and registration." Lucas raised an eyebrow at his brother.

Groaning, Peter reached for his wallet and handed over his license. "I'm late to pick up Fiona. Cut me some slack, will ya?" Leaning over, he flipped open his glove box and dug around for the registration and insurance card.

"Hang tight, I'll be right back."

"Really!" Peter yelled after his brother. He let his head fall back against the seat rest. His own brother was going to give him a speeding ticket. Yeah, he deserved it, but still. He thought being related to the idiot would help.

He counted to ten and then started over when Lucas still hadn't come back to the window. The blue lights were drawing every eye of anyone driving by and... wonderful. There went Mrs. Johnson in her Hummer. Just peachy.

"Okay, I think you've been humbled enough. I'll let you off with a verbal warning. Go have some fun now."

"I'll get you back for this. You know that, right?" Peter snatched his paperwork back and glared at his brother. He could hear Lucas laughing all the way back to his cruiser.

Taking a deep breath, Peter shoved the documents back in the glove box, slammed it closed. Now he was going to be even later. He put his truck in gear and pulled out, ignoring the whoop of the siren as Lucas pulled a U-turn and headed in the other direction.

Peter worked to calm himself as he drove to Fiona's. He didn't need to show up all flustered over Lucas's prank. As he pulled up outside of Fiona's apartment, he noticed a man coming down the walk. Hank. What was he doing here?

He sat in his truck and watched as Hank got into his BMW and slammed the door. Hank smashed his hands against the steering wheel, his face contorted with anger. He started his car and peeled away from the curb.

Hopping out, Peter ran quickly up the walkway to Fiona's apartment. He gave two quick raps on the door. "C'mon..."

Peter stepped back, startled as the door was flung open. "Get out of here before..." Fiona trailed off as she spotted him.

Fiona's face was red, and her fists were balled at her sides. She looked ready to take him out with one punch.

"What happened? Are you okay?" Peter stepped inside and placed his arms on her shoulders. "Are you hurt? What did he do?" He felt his own anger rising. He had a strong urge to go find Henry North III and pummel him into the ground for whatever he had done to Fee.

"It's nothing. I'm fine. It's fine." Fiona stepped back from him, "Come in and give me a minute to freshen up."

Peter took her arm gently to stop her from turning away from him. "What's going on? It's not nothing and you're most definitely not fine. You're shaking. I saw Hank leave. Did he hurt you?"

He resisted the urge to pull her to him. He dipped at the knees so he could look straight into her eyes. "Fee, come on, talk to me."

She sighed and raised a hand to run it through her hair. "Well, happy birthday to me. I forgot I told Hank I would go out with him tonight. I was, well, I was a little distracted this morning after our impromptu breakfast." She gave him a shaky smile. "He's been pestering me to go out ever since he showed up in Haven."

Working to keep his face neutral, Peter pushed the hurt feelings to the back. Just the thought of Fiona agreeing to see someone else made him want to go chase the guy down and do, well, something. Instead, he pushed the thoughts away and walked her to the living room. "Here, sit and tell me what's going on."

They settled side by side on the couch, turning to face each other. Fiona said, "That's just it. I'm not sure what's going on." Fiona leaned a shoulder toward him. Peter put an arm around her and pulled her close.

"Hank came to Haven to find me. He's never denied his past actions. He just discounts it as something 'every man goes through.' But I've made it clear I'm not going back with him. Why won't he leave? There's nothing here for him. I don't understand why he keeps showing up everywhere I go."

"Maybe he'll leave now that he knows you're going out with me. He does know, right?"

Fiona snorted. Peter thought it adorable. "Yeah, he knows. I told him I wasn't going to go out with him tonight. I'd changed my mind. He said some things. I said some things. Then I threatened to call Lucas if he didn't leave."

"That explains why he looked so furious."

"I just don't understand. Hank can have any girl he wants. He's proven that. So, why is he here? He didn't want me enough before, so what's different this time?"

"This isn't very pastor-like of me, but now I want to find Hank and break his nose." Peter took a deep breath. "Fee, you *are* worth it. You just need the right man."

Fiona sat back and looked at him with wide green eyes. He'd done it now. It was too late to back track. "I know this is our first official date, but it's not like we don't know each other, especially not after all this time. Let me just say this..." He reached out and pushed a strand of hair off her face, tucking it behind her ear. "I'm dating with one purpose in mind. One I hope you'll eventually agree to. I'm not taking this relationship lightly, Fee. Not at all. You can trust me."

He leaned forward and pressed a kiss to her forehead. "Let me show you how precious you really are."

Chapter 31

F iona couldn't stop smiling as she remembered her birthday date last night. Granted, it had started out ugly, but it ended beautifully. Peter had been a gentleman all night. The date had been simply perfect.

They'd been seated near a window overlooking the ocean. The lighthouse was off to the side with its light flashing from time to time on its rotation. Ever the gentleman, Peter held her chair for her as she sat.

"I asked for their best table when I made the reservation. This looks close, don't you think?" Peter winked at her as he moved to sit beside her.

"I couldn't imagine better. The view is amazing."

"It couldn't be better."

Fiona caught Peter's eye as he looked directly at her and not out the window. She blushed at the memory even now.

Her heart rate increased with just the thought of how he'd looked at her over his menu last night. She sighed. When Peter went all in on dating, he went all in. She'd pinched herself a time or two over the course of the evening just to make sure she wasn't dreaming. At times it had felt like a fairy tale.

Now, she was headed back to work. She grabbed a jacket and her purse as she walked out the door, locking it behind her. Starting quickly down the sidewalk, she couldn't wipe the smile off her face. She was seeing Peter again tonight. She couldn't wait.

Fiona was looking forward to going to church tomorrow more than she usually did. There was something about knowing she was now dating Peter that made her want to attend and pay attention even more. Maybe she'd try to distract him during his sermon. She laughed out loud. No, that would be mean. Fun. But mean all the same.

Her phone chimed an incoming text, and she pulled it out of her purse to read it.

Munch is STARVING! Can you grab a frosted raspberry hand pie? ASAP? Hurry!

Chuckling, Fiona tapped out a quick reply and quickened her steps. The café was on her way to Seascapes. Fiona wanted to do everything she could to support her friend right now.

The smile slipped as Fiona remembered what Kate had told her a few days ago. Their little one had a congenital heart issue that would need surgery soon after she was born. *Please Lord, spare this child. Heal this little one.* It was a quick prayer she'd started to say whenever she thought about the upcoming birth.

Pushing open the door, Fiona entered the café and hesitated. She spotted Kelsey sitting at the counter having breakfast with Leeann Roberts. Fiona really needed to forgive Kelsey and move on. She also needed to talk with Leeann about the next outing she wanted to do with Sophie. Since Peter was matched with the little girl's brother, they had discussed last night taking them bowling together.

She made her way to the counter near where the ladies were sitting to place her order. "Hello, Leeann, got a minute? I wanted to ask you about taking Sophie out again."

"Sure! She talks a lot about you. She loves having you as her Community Cares friend. It's certainly been a blessing to have someone else spend time with her. My work schedule makes it hard to do anything fun with the kids."

"I think she's adorable. Peter and I were wondering if it would be okay to take the kids bowling in Ellsworth this Saturday."

"Peter?"

"Yeah, since we're matched with the kids, we thought it would be fun to do an outing together."

"Oh, yeah, I guess that's okay."

Fiona frowned, "Is there an issue?"

Leeann flushed. "No, of course not. I just didn't realize you and Peter were..." She trailed off, shooting a quick glance at Kelsey.

"We were what?"

"Well, I thought..." Again, Leeann let her voice trail off.

Kelsey, who had been listening to the conversation, had a puzzled look on her face. "What am I missing?"

"I'm wondering the same thing," Fiona replied.

Leeann turned to face Kelsey. "I saw that post you put up on social media. I thought you were dating Peter."

Kelsey let out a laugh. "Yeah, no. I shut that thread down. I don't know why anyone would think because I posted that photo with Peter and Rocky that the two of us were dating."

Before anyone could say anything else, Brenda bustled up to the counter. "Let me guess. A frosted raspberry hand pie to go?" She raised her eyebrows at Fiona and laughed.

Fiona grinned. "You got it! Munch is apparently *starving*. I'll have one too. Blueberry today if you have it. And a large coffee with two creams. Thanks."

"Munch?" Kelsey looked at her with a puzzled expression. "I haven't heard that name before. Odd isn't it?"

"Oh, that's only what Kate's calling her baby right now," Fiona answered.

"How is Kate doing? I heard the news." Kelsey turned all the way around, with her coffee in hand, to face Fiona.

Fiona worked at being pleasant. She wanted to like Kelsey. It wasn't her fault others had jumped to conclusions, was it?

"They're doing okay. There isn't much they can do until the baby arrives in a few more months." Turning again to look at Leeann, she asked, "So, it's okay to pick up the kids for bowling Saturday?"

"Here you go, sweetie. Tell Kate we're praying for her." Brenda handed over the coffee and pastries. Fiona paid her and turned back to the women.

Leeann smiled, "Sure. Sorry about the confusion. I hope I didn't cause any problems."

"Okay, then we'll be by to pick the kids up at nine on Saturday. I need to get Munch her treat." Glossing over the apology,

Fiona raised the bag slightly and paused when Kelsey gave what seemed to be a genuine smile as she waved goodbye.

Fiona glanced over her shoulder and the two women were chatting and laughing together. She hurried towards Seascapes to give Munch her raspberry hand pie wondering how sincere Kelsey had really been.

Chapter 32

♥

S he's in your office," Kelsey poked her head out and whispered to Peter as he hurried inside the church building. The wind had picked up and he could hear the waves crashing on the beach on this cold March morning.

"Who is?"

"Mrs. Johnson." She grinned mischievously as she raised her nose with an air of superiority.

Peter held back a chortle at Kelsey before he stifled a groan. He'd just finished meeting with Joshua Silverstein about becoming an elder. He was behind on his sermon prep, as usual. He didn't have time to listen to Mrs. Johnson's complaints.

Thankfully, the elder positions were almost filled. Drew had agreed and his meeting with Joshua this morning had confirmed he would be a good fit, too.

And now that Manny was here, he had someone to help with the worship teams. Things were starting to come together and feel less chaotic. The Lord was good.

"Did she say what she wanted?" He spoke quietly so that Mrs. Johnson wouldn't hear him.

"No, she just said she'd wait for you in your office."

Peter grimaced. "Great."

"Good luck," Kelsey smiled sweetly as she handed him a stack of mail.

Peter took a deep breath and pushed open the door to his office. Mrs. Johnson was sitting in a chair in front of his desk, with her large purse in her lap. She was clutching both sides of it, lightly tapping her foot.

"Hello, Mrs. Johnson. Did I miss an appointment with you?"

He knew it was passive-aggressive, but she really needed to stop showing up like this all the time.

"Good morning, young man. I wanted to discuss something with you. I hope you can make time for me in your busy schedule."

The way she said it made it sound like he did nothing all day. Maybe that's exactly what she thought he was doing.

"Absolutely. Unfortunately, I do have other matters I need to work on, so if you can keep this brief?"

"We shall see."

Peter sank into the chair behind his desk. "I do want to let you know that I have spoken with both Joshua Silverstein and my brother, Drew, about becoming elders. They both seem willing. They will let me know their answers soon. I hope you find that agreeable."

The old woman opened her mouth to say something but closed it. He'd never seen Mrs. Johnson at a loss for words. He could get used to this.

"Was there something you wanted to say?"

"That's fine, young man. I'm glad you came to your senses. Now, what about you being pulled over the other evening? I saw you on the side of the road with a police officer's car pulled in behind you."

Peter would really need to get Lucas back now. "That was just my brother playing a prank on me, Mrs. Johnson. Nothing more. If that's all, I really do need to prepare for Sunday."

"There is one more thing, young man. It's about the young lady you've been about town with."

He held up a hand. "Mrs. Johnson, I will hear you out on church related matters whenever you stop by. What I will not do, now or in the future, is listen to any lecture about my personal life."

"Well! Now, see here..."

Peter interrupted her. "No, now if you'll excuse me?" He rose and walked around his desk. Stopping by the chair, he extended a hand towards her. She rose and he escorted her to the door.

"You're making a mistake with that woman. She has far too much passion. It's not going to end well. You mark my words!"

"That's for me to find out, Mrs. Johnson, with all due respect. Now, you have a lovely day."

He shut the door behind him and walked back to his chair. He fell into it and put his head in his hands. He'd never done that to Mrs. Johnson before, and he prayed he wouldn't regret it.

Peter shuffled through the papers on his desk. He really should be better organized. He froze as a white envelope fell to the floor. Not another one. It had been a few weeks, so he'd hoped whoever was leaving them had given up.

He bent slowly to pick it up, wondering if he should just throw it away. No, Lucas had been adamant about being careful with any more he found. Lucas was hoping to get a fingerprint or some other identifying information from it to figure out who was leaving them. Peter left it where it lay on the carpet.

He pulled his cell phone from his pocket and dialed Lucas.

"Hey bro, what's up?"

"Can you come over to the church? I just found another note."

"Did you touch it?" Peter heard the cop switch on in his brother's voice.

"No. I started to, but I stopped. It fell on the floor when I picked up some papers, and I left it there."

"Good. I'll be there in five. Don't touch it."

Peter placed his phone on the desk. He stared at the envelope wondering who it could be. It didn't make sense to him that it was Kelsey, not after what she'd gone through at her last job.

"Lord, please give me clarity on these notes. Help me to figure out who is leaving them. I want them to stop."

His mind wondered back to Fiona. Maybe she *had* been leaving them for him all this time. He sat up and thought about it. It might be possible.

He smiled. The notes took on a whole other meaning if Fiona was the author. He thought back to what was written on them. He made himself wait for Lucas to arrive. He was eager to see what this newest note contained.

Soon he heard footsteps hurrying down the hall towards his office. Peter stood and met his brother at the door.

"Show me." Lucas was focused. He had on a pair of latex gloves and held an evidence bag in his hands.

Peter pointed to where the envelope lay. "What if they're from Fiona?"

Lucas shot him a glance as he bent down to pick it up carefully on the corner. "What makes you say that? Has she told you she left them?"

"No, but it makes sense. Drew said Kate and Fiona have talked about how Fiona wanted to date long before I came to my senses. Maybe she left them so I would ask her out sooner."

"Maybe." Lucas carefully lay the envelope on the desk and used a letter opener he snagged to lift the flap out. He slowly pulled the note out. Peter leaned in to read it over his brother's shoulder.

YOUR EYES DARKEN WHEN YOU LOOK AT ME. IT MAKES MY HEARTBEAT FASTER.

Lucas turned and quirked an eyebrow at his brother. "Does that sound like something Fiona would say to you?"

Peter tried not to blush. He didn't want to give his brother something else to tease him about. "Well, no, not really. But honestly, how would I know? I've spent the last few months trying to avoid Fiona so I wouldn't have all these..." His words died off. He was not going to say the word "feelings" in front of his brother. Nope. Not happening.

"All these what?"

Peter gave his brother a long stare. "What do you feel when you look at Bree?"

A knowing look crossed his brother's face. "Oh, that."

"Yeah, that."

"For how long?"

"I don't want to discuss it. What about the letter?"

"Yeah, I'm going to take this one. I have a buddy at the state crime lab. I'll call in a favor and see if he can get any usable prints off it. You said there were more. Do you still have them?"

"Yeah, but I touched all of those." Peter went around and unlocked his desk draw and pulled out the other two notes. He handed them to his brother.

Lucas dropped them into a separate bag and closed it. "That's okay. Stop by the station Monday and give me a set of your prints. It won't take long."

"Thanks, I appreciate it, Lucas."

Lucas closed the office door behind him as he left. Peter prayed, "Okay, Lord, it would be wonderful if we could find out who those notes are from, but I know You have good plans for me. I'm praying that those notes are from Fiona. I'm praying that You have good plans for us and a future together."

Grabbing his laptop, he walked out the door. He was looking forward to spending the rest of the evening with his girlfriend. His smile widened at the thought. Just a few weeks ago he was committed to being single and now, here he was heading out on a date. God was up there laughing. He was just sure of it.

Chapter 33

♥

F iona was excited for Sunday service in a way she hadn't been in a long time. In fact, she'd started avoiding them. It had been too difficult to see Peter.

Now that Operation Catch a Pastor was a success, she slid into a back pew to watch the worship rehearsal. She hadn't been able to stay home a minute longer. She wanted to see Peter.

"You're here early." Kate slid into the pew next to her, her expanding belly making it difficult for her to move easily. Kate gave out a small sigh when she finally settled next to Fiona.

"You're getting bigger." Fiona smiled to take the sting out.

"I know, isn't it amazing?" Kate smiled and rubbed her hands over her baby bump. "I just hit twenty weeks. Munch is moving and kicking. It's amazing to feel."

The women listened as the worship band started rehearsal. Drew was on stage leading this week with his guitar slung over his shoulder. Peter was playing the keyboard, and Manny was behind the drums. Lucas rounded out the group on the bass guitar.

Kate leaned over to speak in Fiona's ear over the noise. "That much talent in one family should be outlawed." She grinned at Fiona.

"I know, right? Manny seems kind of quiet. I haven't seen him much since he's arrived."

"Yeah, the older brothers were gone by the time Manny was old enough to do a lot with them. I think they're all working on getting to know each other better. Manny seems kind of lost."

Fiona realized she didn't know a whole lot about Peter's family. Maybe when they were together today, she could remedy that. She just knew that the Grant family had taken in lots of foster kids and adopted some of them, including Drew and Manny.

Fiona sat back and enjoyed listening to the men practice the songs. She was here, in church, listening to her boyfriend play. And soon she would listen to her boyfriend preach. She smiled at the word. Boyfriend. She liked how it sounded.

The worship set had a song Fiona hadn't heard before. It had a very upbeat tempo and was the last song. It spoke about lighthouses and how they shine in the darkness. Fiona's foot tapped along.

Jesus really had been her true light over the last year. He'd helped her see Hank's deception before she married him. She wondered where Hank was. She realized she hadn't seen him since he'd stormed out of her apartment a few weeks ago. Well, good riddance. Oops, maybe she shouldn't say something like that in church.

As she read the words to the song on the screen, she felt them deeply in her soul. Jesus had been leading her, even when she hadn't known it. He'd led her to Haven. He'd led her to Kate and her friendship. And most importantly, He'd led her to Peter.

Peter kept his gaze roaming throughout the sanctuary as he delivered his sermon. He didn't let it settle on any one person too long. He searched out those who looked interested in what he had to say. He quickly moved on after making eye contact with Mrs. Johnson sitting with a frown on her face and arms crossed. He lingered for a moment on Joshua Silverstein, who had a studied look on his.

Joshua had confirmed just this morning he would accept the elders position. Drew had done the same a few days before. They once more had a full board.

Peter tried hard not to let his gaze go constantly back to Fiona. Every time he did, he got distracted and fumbled his words. Many wouldn't notice, but he did. His pauses were just a touch too long, or he repeated himself briefly. From the look on Mrs. Johnson's face, she was keeping track to discuss it all with him later.

His eyes flicked past Fiona, resting briefly on Leeann sitting behind her with Brody seated on one side of her and Sophie on the other. The woman had been doing an amazing job at the church for the few short hours she put in each week. The place had never looked so good. Even his office was cleaner than it had ever been. He should probably let her know that.

He brought his mind back to his sermon. He was working on wrapping things up and then they would be singing the song from Rend Collective. It worked perfectly as Peter had planned to speak about how God guides us, just like a lighthouse, in the storms of life.

"Just as Jesus reached out a hand to Peter when the disciples found themselves on a stormed tossed sea," Peter pointed to the stained-glass window showing the story, "He's reaching out a hand to you. You just need to grasp it and let Him guide you.

"It says in Psalm 31:3 'For You are my rock and my fortress; For Your name's sake You will lead me and guide me.

"Let the Lord lead you. He wants to guide you. Cling to Him. Let's pray."

Peter wrapped up the prayer, proud he'd only stumbled once as a stray thought of how Fiona looked this morning popped into his head. He just needed to sing the last song with his brothers before he could take Fiona for a walk on the beach. It was a warm day at the end of March. One of the best kinds in Maine when the promise of spring floated on the salty sea breeze. He couldn't wait to hold her hand as they walked, talking about nothing and everything.

Looking up, he sought Fiona out in the congregation. The song was wrapping up and he wanted to be sure she knew he'd been thinking about her throughout the service.

Fiona smiled at him and blew him a silent kiss. He stumbled slightly, almost falling onto the bench behind the keyboard. He felt his face redden.

He saw his brothers looking at him as well, but he just nodded and placed his hands on the keys to start. Drew shook his head and gave Manny a head bob to start the song.

As the music ramped up, Peter dared a look back at Fiona. Two could play this game. He caught her eye and gave her a wink. He watched the grin widen on her face. He hoped no one else had seen that wink. He dared to look to see if Mrs. Johnson was watching and sure enough, the elderly woman was staring daggers at him.

Peter sighed, but it had been worth it.

Chapter 34

♥

Fiona waited patiently just outside the front door of Seaside Chapel, eager for Peter to finish up and join her for a walk on the beach. She stood off to the side, enjoying the warm breeze, the sunshine, and the fact that Peter had winked at her from the stage.

It had happened so quickly that, if she hadn't had her eyes glued to him, she would have missed it. She noticed a few times when he'd paused during his sermon to look at his notes closely or waited a beat too long to continue. Each moment happened after he locked eyes with her. She had relished each one.

Every time their eyes met, butterflies came to life in her stomach, or her heart sped up slightly. She smiled as she leaned against the railing near the door, waiting for him.

"Hi, Miss Fee!" Sophie skipped up and took Fiona's hand.

Fiona squatted carefully in her high heels, putting herself at eye level with the little girl. "Hi, yourself! Don't you look pretty today!"

Sophie let go of her hand to do a spin, making the skirt on her dress flare out around her under her jacket. "I like how it does that when I spin." She giggled as she stopped and quickly spun again.

"I like it when my skirt does that, too." Fiona stood and did a pirouette beside Sophie, the two giggling at their skirts flaring out.

Fiona stopped, out of breath, thankful this little girl was in her life. She wondered what her own little girl might look like one day. Would she have red hair like hers or dark like...she let the thought trail off as she noticed the women's auxiliary huddled nearby.

Fiona wondered for a moment if she should join them. Most of them were ancient, like Mrs. Johnson. Where was that woman, anyway? She usually tried to snag Peter after service to tell him all the things he'd done wrong.

She wondered if Agnes Johnson had caught the kiss she'd blown Peter or the wink he had given her. If she had, it might be a while before Peter was free for their walk.

"Bye, Miss Fee! I got to go."

Fiona waved at the little girl as she skipped away to grab her mother's hand. Leeann gave her one stern nod before turning her back.

"Ready to go?"

She jumped as Peter whispered in her ear. "Lucky for you I didn't yell. Why are you being so secretive anyway?" Fiona looked over her shoulder and smiled at him.

Peter snagged her hand, pulling her around the corner of the building. "Mrs. Johnson was waiting for me, as usual. Apparently, I was 'too distracted,'" he made air quotes around the words, "during service today. It would be better if I had my mind fully on God during the service and not winking at young women in the congregation."

Fiona couldn't help it. She laughed. "Oh my! What did you say?"

"I agreed with her. I told her, 'Mrs. Johnson, you're absolutely right. My mind was on a certain lady in the audience and if I don't hurry, she's going to leave without me.' Then I turned and walked away before she could say anything else. Probably not my best moment." He shrugged and laughed. "I'll likely hear about that later. And the kiss you blew me certainly didn't help either, you little imp."

Fiona was now laughing so hard she could barely stand. "I wish I could have seen her face!"

Peter tugged her hand, pulling her across the parking lot towards his truck. "If we don't hurry, you just might. C'mon, before she tracks me down to scold me some more. I need to swing by the café. Brenda said she'd have lunch ready for me to pick up."

"Peter! Wait up!"

He gave Fiona a wry look but stopped to wait for Kelsey to catch up with them.

"Sorry," Kelsey grinned at Peter and placed a hand on his arm as she drew near. "It looks like you're headed out. I just wanted to let you know I'll be late on Tuesday."

"Okay, you can just text me next time. No problem. See you then."

Kelsey smiled and turned to head back to the front of the church. Fiona refused to let it bother her though. She trusted Peter. She did.

Peter opened the passenger door for her, and Fiona climbed in. Peter shut the door and jogged around the front. Hopping in, he started the truck and left quickly. "I'm not taking any chances of anyone else stopping me. I can't wait to spend the afternoon with you, Fee."

"Me too, Peter. Me too." She gave him a broad grin.

Peter parked in front of the café, leaving the truck running. "Be right back." He jumped out, walking quickly inside. Fiona smiled, content.

She people watched as she sat waiting. She saw Leeann walking towards the café with Sophie skipping beside and Brody trailing behind. Fiona lifted a hand to wave just as Peter climbed back in and shut the door. Sophie waved back, but Leeann turned and hurried inside.

"That was odd."

"What was odd?" Peter reached across the console between them to take her hand as soon as he'd maneuvered back onto the road.

"What? Oh nothing. Where are we going?" Fiona wasn't sure what she'd seen. She just got the feeling Leeann didn't like her even though it didn't make sense.

"To the lighthouse. I thought it appropriate after my sermon today. Too corny?"

Fiona smiled at him. "Not corny at all. I love the lighthouse. I can see it from my apartment. It always brings me comfort, especially knowing how long it's been there, saving all those lives over the years. It's such a symbol of hope, isn't it?"

He squeezed her hand. "I like that. Hope."

They continued towards the beach. Fiona watched the passing scenery. Haven in the spring was one of her favorite times. And now, with Peter beside her, it was even more perfect.

"What was odd earlier?"

"Oh, it was nothing. Honest."

"If it was really nothing, then just tell me."

Fiona looked at him. "Okay." She drew out the word and squeezed his hand. "When you got in the truck, I noticed Leeann walking towards us with her kids. I waved but she just stared right through me. I just found it, well, odd."

"Maybe she didn't see you. Her mind could have been on something else."

"Maybe. I hope it doesn't have anything to do with me mentoring Sophie."

"I'm sure it was nothing. Maybe the sun was in her eyes, so she didn't see you through the glare on the window."

Fiona left it alone. Maybe Leeann Roberts didn't like her. Maybe she was still thought Kelsey wanted to date Peter. She was at least a loyal friend to Kelsey.

Chapter 35

♥

As the afternoon wore on, Peter was glad for his Sunday afternoons off. He lay back against the boulder he and Fiona were using as a table, his eyes closed against the sun. He thought springtime in Haven was one of the best seasons. It made the winter months all worth it. When the first warm day hit, people flocked to the beach to walk and enjoy the sunshine.

In fact, he could hear a few people even now walking the paths above. He'd brought Fiona to his favorite hidden spot on the shore to watch the water. Cracking an eye, he turned his head to watch her instead.

She wore a wide brimmed hat shading her pale complexion from the sun. She was leaning back against the boulder beside him, within arm's reach if he wanted to touch her. He decided he did and took her hand. She lazily turned her head and smiled at him.

On impulse, he asked, "Tell me, is it true?"

"Is what true?" She smiled at him again.

How he loved her smile. And her green eyes, the color of new spring leaves. When she looked at him, sometimes they darkened a little.

"Do my eyes darken when I look at you? Is your heart beating faster?" He turned to her as he asked the questions.

Confusion crossed Fiona's face. "I don't know. I think so."

"You wrote all that in the last note you left for me." He held his breath as he waited to see if she would confirm she had indeed written the notes he'd been finding.

Fiona stared at him. "Peter, what are you talking about? What notes?"

He sat up away from the boulder as he tried to explain. "The notes you've been leaving for me in my office. The ones telling me how you feel about me. You left them to convince me to start dating, right?" Peter started to have a sinking feeling in his stomach as he continued to speak.

"Peter, I have no idea what you're talking about. What notes?"

He couldn't seem to stop the words. "You've been sneaking into my office, right? Did Kelsey help or was it Drew?"

"I haven't been sneaking into your office." Fiona pulled her hand free, raising an eyebrow at him.

He should have kept his mouth shut, but it was too late to take his words back now. He'd promised her honesty. He swallowed hard as he continued, "I've been finding these notes over the last couple of months. They've been saying things like 'Your eyes darken when you look at me. It makes my heartbeat faster.' I was hoping, well, I thought they might be from you."

Fiona stared at him with her mouth open in shock. "You think *I* left you these notes?"

"Yeah. I, just thought, maybe you'd left them to convince me to date you. They didn't start showing up until I decided I was going to only focus on God and the church." He chuckled, trying to ease the tension. "And look, it worked!"

"It's not me! How could you think I would play a game like that with you?"

Fiona stood and started picking her way barefoot carefully down the boulders towards the beach, her high heels swinging from one hand.

"Where are you going?" He scrambled up to follow.

"I need to walk."

Fiona hit the sand before Peter had cleared the last obstacle to the beach and took off at a fast pace. He had to jog to catch up with her.

She whirled at him as he came up beside her. Her eyes sparking at him. "It's not me. So, who is it, Peter? Why would someone leave you a note like that? What have you been doing?"

"I have no idea, Fiona. I just told you that. I asked Lucas to investigate them. He came yesterday when I found the newest one. He sent it to a buddy at the crime lab to see if they could get any fingerprints off it."

"If you thought I'd left them, why didn't you just ask me? Did you really think they were from me? If you did, you certainly wouldn't have sent them off for fingerprinting. What's really going on, Peter?"

Peter worked to keep the frustration out of his voice as he heard the anger in Fiona's. It wasn't her fault that someone was leaving him notes. It also wasn't his.

"Okay, let's just take a minute. First, I'm sorry. I was hoping it was you. But you're right, you would have just told me. You *did* tell me how you felt, but I ignored it. Now I don't know what to do. I have no idea who it could be."

"Kelsey." The name slipped out of Fiona's mouth, and she looked away quickly.

"It's not Kelsey."

She turned back to him. "How can you be so sure? She has access to your office. It would be easy to leave notes without you seeing her." He heard the jealousy in her voice and saw her eyes blazing with anger.

Fiona once more started to walk away. Peter snagged her elbow to stop her. His own anger was beginning to rise. He hadn't done anything wrong here. He turned her to face him.

"Don't be mad at me. Please. It's not my fault. It's no one's fault." He stared into her eyes. "I only have eyes for you. Just you." He tried to gauge how mad she still was.

Fiona refused to meet his gaze. He could see the anger, but jealousy as well.

"Don't shut me out. Talk to me, Fee. "

"I swore I would never feel this way again, Peter. Never again. This relationship has no chance of moving forward if I can't trust you."

He tightened his grip on her hand. "Fee, I'm trying to tell you just how much you mean to me. And you *can* trust me."

Emotions stormed across Fiona's face.

Peter took a breath before continuing, "Fee, I've told you I have no idea who left me the notes. I've told you I'm sorry. I've told you how much you mean to me. What else can I do?"

It took a lot to make Peter angry, but he didn't understand this. He was being accused of something, but he didn't know what. He wasn't liking it. Not one bit.

"Let me drive you home before we say something we both might regret." Peter turned and started back towards the boulders to gather their picnic supplies.

Fiona didn't move. "Unless you can tell me how those notes got on your desk, don't bother coming. Don't bother calling. I don't want to hear your excuses."

"See that's what I meant. Things we would regret," Peter sighed as he felt his anger fade. This wasn't how he wanted things to be. They had only just started dating. He had prayed this relationship would become more. Maybe he had misheard God after all.

"C'mon, let's go and I'll bring you home. We can finish this later when we've both calmed down."

"No, thanks. I think I'll just walk home." She spun on her heel and hurried, still barefoot across the cold sand, back towards the lighthouse.

Peter turned to the woman he loved, opening his mouth to speak. He paused as he watched her practically run away from him. Had he ever told her that?

He realized in this moment, that he did love Fiona. In fact, he had ever since their dance lessons. He'd just been too scared to act on it. And now it might be too late. He needed to figure out who was leaving the notes and get this sorted. And fast.

As he drove home, he thought back to the first moment he'd seen Fiona Gilliam. He remembered how his heart had fluttered in his chest and how he hadn't been able to put two words together coherently. He remembered the months when he had been focused solely on the church. Months when he could have been dating her, getting to know her better. Now he might lose all of it over notes left by a secret admirer.

If she didn't trust his word, how could they stay together? "Lord, make my path clear. Help me figure out what it is you want me to do and open the doors for me."

Peter trailed off and began to contemplate what he should be doing. Because right now, he had no idea.

Chapter 36

♥

F iona stomped into her apartment, slamming the door behind her. The nerve of that man! He obviously was doing *something* to encourage *someone*. Why else would he have notes like that? It didn't make sense.

She kicked her shoes off. The thumps they made against the wall were satisfying. She padded into the kitchen in her bare feet, opened the freezer door, and grabbed a pint of mint chocolate chip ice-cream. Her favorite. She didn't even bother with a bowl. Grabbing a spoon and her phone, she dropped onto the couch.

Fiona popped a spoonful of the ice-cream into her mouth and typed out a text to Kate. Maybe she could help her make sense of it all.

I had a fight with Peter. And I'm still mad at him.

What happened?

Someone has been leaving him love notes on his desk. He says he doesn't know who or why. C'mon! He thought it was me!

And it wasn't. So what happened?

I got mad and walked home from the lighthouse.

What are you going to do now?

Eat ice-cream and pout. What else?

Call Peter and talk to him? That might be a better plan.

Kate! I thought you'd be on my side!

Fiona tossed the phone on to the couch and took another spoonful of the ice-cream. How could Kate side with Peter? Maybe because she was married to Drew now, she felt like she had to stick with family.

Fiona heard her phone ding. She stuck another spoonful of ice-cream in her mouth before picking it up.

Fee, I am on your side. You're blowing it out of proportion. It's not Peter's fault someone left notes on his desk. Maybe you should help him figure out who did it so he can address how inappropriate it was instead of being mad. Any ideas who did it?

Fiona stared blankly out the window at the lighthouse. It had to be Kelsey.

Kelsey. Especially after that post.

Peter wouldn't cheat on you, Fee. Call him!

Sighing, Fiona took another bite of ice-cream, although she was losing her appetite for it. She knew she'd let her temper get the best of her...again. Her mother had always warned her to keep it under tight reins.

The thought of Peter cheating on her and denying it – just like Hank – had thrown her into a tailspin.

Picking up her phone again, she decided to call Grandma Josie. She needed more advice on this. She sent another text to Kate first.

Talk to you soon. Going to call Gram.

Call Peter after. :-)

I'll consider it. I think I need to make him suffer longer first. :-)

Be wise, Fee. Don't make him suffer for something he didn't do.

Fiona looked at the words from Kate. She felt her anger cooling. She was doing that, wasn't she?

Sighing, she tapped on the shortcut for her grandmother. Bringing the phone to her ear, she listened as it rang – once...twice. She tapped her toe with impatience as she waited for Grandma Josie to answer.

"Hello?"

"Hi, Gram, it's me, Fiona. How are you doing?"

"Hi, honey. I'm good. Susan's been checking on me. How are things going with that man of yours?"

"That's why I'm calling. I need some advice. Got a minute?"

"Sure do, sweetie. Tell me what's going on."

Fiona's heart swelled at the sound of Grandma Josie's voice. She knew how blessed she was to have the family she did. She'd realized this even more so after being friends with Kate.

"Well, we started dating, like I hoped we would when I went home."

"What's the problem then? You have a spat?"

"You could say that. I think I might have let my temper get in the way." Fiona sighed as she filled her grandmother in on what happened leading up to her losing her cool. Grandma Josie listened attentively, asking clarifying questions as they went.

"Well, dear, I think you may have overreacted, but it's not the end of the world. Go tell that man you're sorry and move forward."

"So, I shouldn't worry about the notes?"

"I wouldn't. Not yet anyway. Not every man is like Hank, dear. There are some good ones out there. Who knows how the notes got there? Don't borrow trouble. Has Peter ever lied to you before?"

"No, not that I know of anyway."

"Why do you think he's lying now?"

"I don't know. But if he wasn't encouraging someone else, why would he be getting the notes? It's such a mess, Gram."

"No, it isn't. It's an inconvenience. It's only a mess if you can't fix it. This you can fix. Get off the phone, go find him, and make it right. If you think he's worth the trouble, go to the trouble to make it better."

Fiona felt a tug in her spirit at her grandmother's words. She'd certainly made a mess of things and she needed to fix it. "Thanks, Gram. I'm going to go find, Peter. I'll let you know what happens."

"Thanks, sweetie. Love you. Bye."

"Love you too." Fiona tapped the off button to end the call. She got up and replaced the slightly melted ice-cream in the freezer and put the spoon in the sink. She had a man to go find.

Smiling to herself, she went to her bedroom to fix her makeup and hair. She wanted to look her best for this.

Chapter 37

♥

P eter's head was still spinning from yesterday's events. He wasn't sure if he'd ever win Fiona back. Not after she'd walked home, barefoot even, from their fight yesterday.

He'd gone for a long drive along the coast instead of going straight home. As he drove, he thought back to all the good times with Fee. Her laughter. Her eyes. Her hair. Everything about her was so captivating, but was it enough to hold his heart?

The fun they'd had during dance lessons could still bring a smile to his face. He'd been so scared to try and yet, she'd coaxed him and encouraged him enough that he'd succeeded without making a fool of himself.

It was the thought of losing her that made him pull over into an empty parking lot and pray. "Lord, You have a plan for my life. I trust You. I fully trust in all You're doing. I know it's for my own good and not for harm. Even though it's felt harmful lately." Taking a deep breath, he continued, "And if not having Fiona in my life is part of Your plan, help me to accept it. Help me to see the goodness in it all. Because right now, it doesn't feel good. It hurts, Lord."

Now, here he was, waiting on God's timing, while he worked on finishing up the last bits and pieces of his home renovation. Peter measured around the bottom of his bedroom window, marking measurements for trim.

His heart was settled. He'd felt God tell him to wait. Wait for Fiona.

Walking outside to cut the trim board he needed, he stopped short on the porch when he saw Fiona stepping out of her car. He'd called her when he'd gotten home last night, hoping she was ready to talk. She hadn't answered her phone. He'd left a message, once more apologizing for upsetting her.

This morning, he sent a text asking to see her today. She didn't respond. Now, here she was.

Pushing his hands into his pockets, he stood rocking on his feet. *Lord, please let us be able to work this, whatever this is, out. I don't want to lose her before I even have her. But help me accept whatever happens next.*

"I brought a peace offering." Peter looked at the bag of pastries she held up with the Three Cat Café logo stamped on the side. "Can we talk? Maybe go sit on the beach?"

"Sure, let me grab a jacket. Do you have coffee, or should I grab us some from inside?"

Leaning back into her car, she brought out a drink carrier. Holding it up, she said, "I brought coffee." She smiled tentatively at him.

Peter reached inside the door to snag a light jacket from a hook. The sun was shining, and it was warm enough working in a t-shirt going in and out, but the beach would be cooler.

They picked their way down the path to the sand, not talking. At the bottom, Fiona turned to him and began to speak, "Peter, I..."

He placed a finger on her lips to quiet her. "Hold that thought. Come with me." He took the cup holder from her and took her hand, tugging her to follow him.

He led her to where he'd set up a rough bench a few weeks ago. There was a sanded plank on two boulders that were close enough in size to make sitting there comfortable. He waved a hand towards it, "Have a seat."

Fiona settled on the bench. He sat beside her, placing the drink carrier between them.

Turning, so she could see him, she said, "Peter, I wanted to apologize for how I acted yesterday." She met his eyes. "I overreacted and, well, I'm sorry." She reached into the pastry bag and handed him a frosted raspberry hand pie. "Forgive me?"

Peter looked at the hand pie and then into her eyes. He saw her eyes dim when he hesitated in taking the pastry. He smiled as he reached for it. "Forgiven."

They sat quietly side by side, eating their treats and sipping their coffee. Fiona took her last bite before turning to face him. "Peter, there's one thing you should know about me. It's kind of important."

She looked so earnest facing him. His gut clenched. She'd asked for forgiveness, but maybe she'd decided she didn't want to pursue a relationship. Maybe friendship was all she really wanted.

Placing the drink carrier on the sand, he scooted closer. He took her hand in his. "You can tell me anything." He squeezed her hand, praying she wasn't going to walk away for good.

"Well, you see, I have this temper."

"You don't say?" Peter quirked an eyebrow at her. Fiona laughed.

"Are you going to let me say what I want to say?"

"I'm not stopping you, sweetheart."

Her green eyes shot up to look deeply into his brown ones at the term of endearment. It felt good to call her that.

Letting go of his hand, Fiona rose to her feet and stood in front of him. "I'm sorry I let my temper get the best of me. I'm so sorry I didn't trust you, and I got mad about the notes. I know it's not your fault they keep showing up. I'm sorry I walked away and wouldn't listen to you."

"I've already forgiven you."

"I know, but I wanted to make sure you really understand. I *do* trust you."

Peter rose slowly, taking both her hands in his. "I'm so glad," he said in a husky voice filled with thankfulness at her words. Leaning forward with his eyes fixed on her lips, he knew it was time to kiss her. He wanted to show her what she truly meant to him.

Just as their lips began to touch, there was a raucous cry and two seagulls swooped down behind them on the bench. They began fighting over the hand pie he hadn't finished.

Laughing, the couple sprang apart. Peter ran at the birds, flapping his arms to scare them off. He heard Fiona's laughter ringing out behind him. Snatching up his trash, he stuffed it in a coat pocket.

"Where were we?" He walked with determination towards Fiona. Now that he could kiss her, he wanted nothing more than to feel her lips under his.

"Right about here, if I remember right." Fiona's laughter faded but she still had a grin on her face. She grabbed his jacket collar with both hands and pulled him down towards her.

He should slow things down, he thought, just as their lips met. Then all thought ceased to exist. He had the woman he loved in his arms. He'd waited far too long for this moment.

"Peter!"

He groaned as he pulled back.

Looking up, he saw Manny standing at the top of the path, waving his arms at him. "I need you!"

"So do I," Fiona whispered as she dropped her head to his chest.

"Remind me to have a talk with my younger brother about appropriate interruptions, will you?"

Peter took her hand and started walking towards the path back up. "Can I take you out later tonight?"

"I'd love that."

Holding hands, they made their way back up to the top of the path. Manny waited for them, with a look of chagrin on his face.

"So, what's so important, little brother?" Peter raised an eyebrow at Manny.

"Um, I couldn't find the remote and the Rays game was about to start. I'm sorry! I didn't realize, well, I didn't realize..."

Manny's voice trailed off as his eyes darted between Peter and Fiona. "I'm an idiot."

Sighing, Peter turned to Fiona. "I'll see you tonight. I'm going to go put this one to work as penance."

Fiona giggled as Peter kissed her on the cheek before she got in the car.

Turning to Manny, he growled, "C'mon you lug head. Let's go find the remote." Peter grabbed his brother in a headlock and dragged him inside.

Peter had a hard time keeping his mind focused at work the next day. Fiona's face kept popping up and distracting him. He smiled as he picked up a stack of papers to look for where he'd jotted some references he wanted to use. A pink slip of paper was nestled in the stack. He didn't use pink paper.

He fished the paper out and dropped it like it was on fire.

I LOVE THE WAY YOUR HAND
FEELS ON MY ARM.

Good Lord in heaven, he thought. *This needs to stop.*

He walked to the door, making sure it was firmly closed. He glanced at the lock, considering. He'd never felt the need to lock the door before. He left it and went back to his desk.

Sinking into his chair, he glared at the note where it lay on his desk. He picked it up at the corner with his forefinger and thumb. He needed to get these notes to stop.

Scowling, he crumpled the note and threw it in the trash bin beside his desk. He stared at it for a moment before sighing and pulling it back out. He smoothed it, regarding the words once more.

The only person he'd touched recently was Fiona. He tried to remember if he'd touched anyone else – someone who might leave a note like this. He came up with nothing.

Sighing, he pulled an envelope out of a drawer and placed the note inside.

I got another note. He tapped the blue arrow to send the text to Lucas.

Setting the note aside, he shuffled the papers again, looking for the list of references. Finding it, he attempted to go back to working on the sermon. He tried to focus, but his brain wouldn't stop processing who might be sending the notes. He put his head on his desk.

"Lord, a little help with this would be fantastic."

His phone dinged for an incoming text. Picking it up, he read Lucas's reply. *I'm at the Three Cats. Want me to come to you or do you want to meet me here?*

Peter stared at what he'd written so far for his sermon. He shook his head. It was no good. All he could think about were the notes. He sent a quick text back to Lucas. *I'm coming. Order me something.*

He shoved his laptop in his bag along with his sermon notes. Grabbing his keys and the envelope, he headed for his truck, praying Lucas would have answers.

Peter pulled into a parking spot next to Lucas's cruiser. He grabbed the note and hurried inside. His brother was sitting at the counter flirting with Bree.

He slid onto the stool beside Lucas, lightly bumping him in the shoulder with his own. "Hey, what did you get me?"

"Well, my fabulous and gorgeous wife here saved us two cinnamon rolls." Lucas winked at Bree. She laughed and swatted at him. "She even says a fresh pot of coffee is coming."

"It's right here, you big lout." Bree chuckled as she pulled two cups from under the counter. Turning, she grabbed the hot pot of coffee and poured each man a cup. "Cream and sugar are right there."

"Ha! We drink it like real men, black like it should be." Lucas lifted the steaming cup to his lips and took a sip. He winced. "But we might let it cool down before doing that again." He winked once more at his wife as she laughed and walked away to tend to other customers.

Peter smiled at the banter. He wanted more of that with Fee and less of the angry fireworks from the other day. He handed the envelope with the note to Lucas. "Here's the newest one. There was no envelope this time, just the note."

Lucas pulled the note out and read it. "I still haven't heard from my buddy at the crime lab. This makes four, right?"

"Yeah." Peter took a bite of his cinnamon bun. It was worth being behind on his sermon this week just for one taste of this divine deliciousness.

"It looks like it's just someone who has the hots for you. I'm not really concerned since none of them seem threatening. I'm not sure there's much more we can do."

"Right." Peter sipped his coffee. None of them did seem threatening, but he felt as if there was something else behind the notes. He just wished he knew who it was so he could stop it.

Unless Lucas could help him, Peter didn't know what to do next.

Chapter 38

♥

F iona yawned as she stretched her arms overhead. She'd arrived at work early to get a jumpstart on a few projects. She was putting together an intricate design on a jewelry set requiring a lot of close work.

The necklace and matching earrings would be lovely once completed. She was working on lining the glass with wire rather than wrapping it. She liked the way it showed off the sea glass better, but it hurt her eyes when she worked too long on it.

She'd also been out late celebrating with Bree and Lucas. The two had celebrated their wedding with all their family and friends. It was the original date they'd planned to get married.

Even though Bree and Lucas were already married, the ceremony had still been touching. The love the couple had for each other had been evident throughout the evening.

Walking behind the counter, she picked up her phone and her coffee. She went to the back room to heat up her beverage and mindlessly opened her favorite social media app. She began thumbing through the feed as she waited for the microwave.

The microwave beeped. Taking her coffee out, Fiona leaned with her back against the counter and continued scrolling, sipping her warm coffee.

She froze. She'd just thumbed up to a post that showed a picture of Peter behind the pulpit. He looked like he was in mid-sermon. The text read *Peter Grant is one of the most desirable men in Haven. I'm so glad he's mine.*

Mouth open in shock, Fiona flipped through the rest of the photos. They included Peter walking on the beach alone, bent over his desk reading something, and playing the keyboard in church.

What on earth? Fiona stood straight up, away from the counter. She clenched her jaw with anger. It wasn't her post and, last she checked, Peter Grant was all hers.

Kelsey. It had to be Kelsey. So much for thinking her last post was a mistake.

Oh gosh. Fiona's mouth dropped open again. It wasn't Kelsey. It was Leeann Roberts! She looked again to see if anyone had commented or liked the photo.

Sure enough, there were several comments as well as a few thumbs up and hearts. She tapped to open the comment section and began reading.

So happy for you, Leeann! You deserve it!

"No, she doesn't," Fiona growled under her breath. "She's lying!"

What a hottie! Where did you find him?

"Back off! He's my hottie!" Fiona muttered.

Wow! He's gorgeous! Does he have any brothers?

"He does, but they're all taken too! Sheesh!" Fiona felt herself growing angrier as she continued to read. There were more than a dozen congratulating Leeann on her new "relationship."

Fiona felt her face flaming with temper. She forced herself to put her coffee down and take some deep breaths. She worked to ease the grip she had on her phone. This wasn't happening. Where did this woman get off lying like this?

She stopped. The notes. The post. Leeann.

She snapped a screenshot before texting Peter. *Where are you?*

Fiona tapped her foot impatiently as she waited for his reply. The back door opened and in walked Kate. "Hi, Fee..." Her voice trailed off. "What's wrong?"

"This!" Fiona pulled up the post again and pushed her phone forward to show it to Kate.

"Woah. Hang on a second." Kate took the phone gently and scanned the post.

"Read the comments while you're there. How could she? What does she think she's doing anyway? The nerve!"

"Slow down, Fee. Let's get all the facts first."

Fiona glared at her friend with eyes narrowed. "Facts? Here are the facts. One," Fiona held up a finger, "she makes this totally inappropriate post. Let's not forget, totally *wrong* post. Peter is *not* hers. Not unless something happened in the middle of the night to change anything."

"I know, Fee. I know. But..."

Fiona continued as if she hadn't heard Kate trying to talk. "Two," another finger went up, "she's been leaving notes in Peter's office. It's got to be her, Kate. She's cleaning the church.

She must have access to his office when no one is looking. And all along I thought it was Kelsey. I'm going to..."

"You're going to calm down. Deep breaths with me. Look at me, Fee." She waited for Fiona to make eye contact with her. "You know I'm with you in whatever you do, but let's look at this rationally before you go off and grab a baseball bat or something. Drew isn't going to be happy if he has to bail us out of jail for attacking the woman."

Before Fiona could answer, she heard her phone ding. Pulling it out of Kate's grasp, she snatched it back. *I'm at the church. The women's aux is here planning some big summer festival and wanted my input. Save me!*

Fiona snorted. She quickly tapped out her response. *Is Leeann there?*

Yes. Why?

I'm on my way. Don't let her leave. Fiona attached the screenshot of Leeann's post.

"You'd better come with me. I'm going to go confront Leeann with this." She shook her phone at Kate. "Whatever 'this' is. Shoot. I forgot we didn't have anyone else in the store today. No, stay here. Peter will hold me back, I'm sure."

Kate shot her friend a look. "Do you honestly think I'm going to wait here while you go deal with this? Fat chance. I'm coming with you. And I'm driving." Kate snatched up her keys. "Go lock the front door."

"She's going to regret the day she thought she could have Peter." She ran back through the store, threw the deadbolt, and flipped over the closed sign.

Fiona sprinted back through the store. She knew there was no substance to Leeann's claim, but what kind of woman did that?

It didn't matter. Fiona was going to put a stop to it. And she hoped she wouldn't need anyone to bail her out of jail.

Chapter 39

Peter stared in horror at the text Fiona had just sent. He looked up and scanned the room. Leeann was seated at the table with her back to him. Mrs. Johnson was at the front of the room laying out her ideas for the summer festival.

He shot a text off to Lucas. *I think Leeann left the notes.* He attached the screenshot and waited.

I know. On my way.

What did that mean? *Did your buddy get back to you?*

Yup.

And? Peter wanted to shake the information out of his brother.

I'll be there in less than 5. Don't let her leave.

Peter huffed as he slid his phone into his front pocket. Mrs. Harris turned and placed a lip to her fingers to shush him. "Sorry," he mouthed.

How was he going to stop Leeann from leaving? Especially in front of a room full of other women.

Leeann. It had been Leeann Roberts all along. Quiet Leeann with two adorable little children. No husband. No boyfriend. And he'd never found out why. It was a slippery slope for a single man, especially if he was a pastor, to learn more about the single women in church. He had to be careful he didn't give off the wrong impression.

He stiffened as Leeann glanced over her shoulder at him and smiled before turning back to the front. Oh no. Had he given *her* the wrong impression? He racked his brain for all the moments he'd spoken to her.

He talked to her when he picked up Brody for their outings. He didn't think he'd ever given off the wrong idea. Had he?

He heard gravel spewing as a car came into the parking lot fast. Peter stepped up behind Mrs. Harris, speaking quietly in her ear. "I need to go check on something. If anyone has any questions, I'll answer them when I get back."

She just nodded to let him know she'd heard him. Mrs. Johnson was on a roll, and she didn't give up the spotlight easily.

Peter slipped out the door and hurried to meet Lucas. His brother was just walking in the back door with Fiona and Kate hot on his heels. Peter swallowed hard. He could almost see steam rolling off Fiona. She was gorgeous when she was mad.

"What does she think she's doing? Is she in there?" Fiona shoved past Lucas and started towards the fellowship hall where the meeting was being held.

"Nope. Hold it." Lucas snatched Fiona's arm and pulled her to a stop. "Listen. We need to handle this carefully. I don't want it to get out of hand. Fiona, go wait in Peter's office with Kate."

"Ha! Fat chance of that happening." Fiona stood with arms crossed, facing off against Lucas. "I won't go drag her out here and demand answers, but I'm not going anywhere." Peter held back a smile. He thought her look of defiance was utterly adorable, but he didn't think she would appreciate that right now. And he didn't want that fire aimed in his direction.

"Fine. Peter," Lucas pointed at his brother, "your job is to simply make sure Fiona doesn't go after Leeann. Let me handle this."

Peter nodded his head and quickly stepped up beside Fiona. "Are you mad at me?" He reached to take her hand. She allowed him to pull her into his side.

"Not at you. Although I'm getting a bit tired of the women in this town thinking they're dating you. It might be time for you to do a press release. Let the town know the single pastor is no longer available. Just so no one else gets any ideas." She gave him a tight smile and squeezed his hand.

Lucas took charge. "Kate, do you mind going in and asking Leeann to come out here? I'd rather not cuff her in front of everyone if we can manage it."

"Cuff her?" Peter looked at his brother with confusion. "What has she done that warrants that? It was just a few notes. I'm sure we can have a conversation about how it's inappropriate and move on from there."

"It's not about the notes. When my buddy found her print, we knew it was her because she was already in the system. She has an outstanding warrant. She kidnapped her children. Her ex-husband has full custody."

Peter gaped at his brother. "She what? Wait. Is it safe for Kate to go get her?"

Kate looked between her two brothers-in-law. At that moment the back door opened and in walked Drew and Manny. Kate sighed and hurried to her husband.

"Want to fill me in? Kate texted me that something was happening at the church, and you might need me." Drew pulled his wife close as he waited for one of his brothers to answer him.

Lucas said, "In a minute, Drew. How much time before the meeting is over, Peter?"

Peter turned to Lucas. "Um, I don't know. Mrs. Johnson was talking when I left. It could be ten minutes it could be thirty. It's hard to tell."

"Okay." Lucas nodded his head. "Here's what we'll do. Drew, you and Manny go in the sanctuary and make sure no one goes out or comes in that way. Lock the front doors."

"You got it. Kate, you're coming with me." Drew took his wife's hand and started to tug her along.

"But Lucas wanted me to go get Leeann."

Drew shot his brother a glare. "Not happening. C'mon." Drew didn't wait for Lucas to counter him. He towed Kate behind him as Manny followed the couple.

"Okay, now Peter, go back in there. Tell the women there's an emergency that has come up. They need to leave. Make something up. As they start to go, ask Leeann to meet you in your office. Fiona and I will be in there waiting. Got it?"

Peter shook his head. Things were happening so fast. He was still wrapping his head around the fact that Leeann had a warrant out for kidnapping her own children. That she'd left the notes for him paled in comparison.

"Peter? We can't waste much more time. I already called for a social worker and the chief to pick up the kids from school. I need to get Leeann into custody soon before..."

Lucas broke off as the door to the fellowship hall banged open and Leeann came running into the hall. She stopped when she saw the three of them standing there.

Lucas held up a hand and started forward. "Leeann, you need to come with me."

Leeann looked wildly around. The fellowship hall was filled with women standing around and chatting. Peter, Fiona, and Lucas were blocking the back door. Leeann's eyes darted towards the sanctuary door.

Lucas took another slow step towards the woman. "Don't run, Leeann. It's too late. You need to come with me. It will look better to the judge if you cooperate."

After only a moment's hesitation, Leeann's shoulders sagged. "I give up." She held out her hands to Lucas.

Lucas walked forward, turning her around to place a pair of handcuffs. He started reading her rights to her as he frisked her. As soon as he was done, he started walking her toward the door.

"What do you think you're doing, young man?"

The wide-eyed women from the auxiliary were all gathered in the doorway. Mrs. Johnson was at the front and looked ready to thump someone on the head with her cane. "Unhand her at once!"

"This is a police matter, Mrs. Johnson. Please, step back." Lucas shot an apologetic look at his brother at leaving him to deal with Mrs. Johnson before continuing out the door with Leeann.

Mrs. Johnson turned her furious gaze at Peter. "I thought you'd made progress here. I was ready to support you. But this! This is more than I think any church can bear. Why was this poor woman arrested on church property? Isn't this a place of sanctuary?"

The stream of words rolled off Peter's back. He wasn't sure he could explain. He was still trying to understand it himself.

Fiona stepped forward. "Ladies, please. Leeann made a bad choice. A really bad choice, and it caught up to her today. Lucas had to arrest her. He had to. If you want more details than that, maybe you could visit Leeann and have her tell you her side. I think she's going to need all the support she can get."

Fiona finished addressing the women and turned to Peter. "Let's get out of here."

Peter gave her a quick smile and took her hand. They walked out the door together, as he ignored the squawking from Mrs. Johnson, still demanding answers.

"Hold up just a second." Fiona pulled out her phone. "Just wanted to let Kate and the rest know it was safe to come out. Is the church okay if you leave?"

"Yeah. Drew can lock up. Let's go."

Peter pulled her towards his truck and opened her door. "Fiona."

She turned to look at him. She was standing between the door and Peter. He reached out and cupped her cheek with a hand. "Thank you. Thank you for believing me." Leaning in, he brushed her cheek with a kiss. "Let's go."

She smiled at him before climbing in. He wasn't sure what he would end up preaching this week, but he knew God had his back. As always.

Chapter 40

♥

F iona took a deep breath of the salty ocean air. She loved
her walk to work along the boardwalk. It was one of the
best things about living in Haven. So much had happened
over the course of the last week that she was still working to
process it all.

Leeann confessed to everything once Lucas had her at
the station. She'd lived in Iowa. Her husband traveled a lot
for his job. He'd arrived home early once and caught her
cheating. And it wasn't the first time either.

During the divorce, he'd also shown her inability to prop-
erly care for their children. She admitted to not being a great
mother before the divorce. Fiona didn't remember seeing
anything when she'd been out with Sophie that made her
think Leeann wasn't a good mom. Leeann assured Lucas
she'd changed.

It didn't matter though. Her ex-husband had full custody
of the children. On Leeann's last visit with them, she'd
simply never returned them. Dan Roberts had been looking
for them since last fall.

Dan flew in to pick them up as soon as he was notified. He was thankful to be reunited with his children. Sophie and Brody seemed happy to see their father as well.

Sophie had even brought her father to Seascapes to introduce him to Fiona. The little girl introduced Fiona as her "most favorite sledder ever!" Fiona laughed now at the memory.

She couldn't get over the fact that if Leeann had never left those notes for Peter, it was likely she wouldn't have been found.

Her ringing cell phone brought her out of her musings. She dug it out of her purse. She didn't recognize the number, but still answered. "Hello, this is Fiona."

"Fiona, this is Agatha North. I want to know the location of Henry. Where is he?"

Fiona took the phone away from her ear and looked at it in confusion.

"Hello? Are you there?"

"I'm sorry. I have no idea where your son is, Agatha. I haven't seen him in weeks." Fiona was startled to realize that was true. She hadn't seen him since the night he'd arrived for the date that never happened. He must have finally decided to leave her alone. She was so caught up with being with Peter, she'd put Hank out of her mind.

"Well, the last location I had for him was with you. I do not have time for games. Tell me where he is, right now."

Fiona pulled the phone away from her ear again and glared at it. Returning it to her ear, she said in a steady, but steely tone, "Look Agatha. I haven't seen your son. Why don't you call him?

I don't know why you would even think I would know where he was. We aren't together anymore. You know that."

"He was given specific instructions. I thought he went to carry them out, but it looks like he has not. How disappointing."

"And what instructions were those?" Fiona asked with curiosity, not expecting an answer.

"He was to marry you."

Fiona shook her head. She must have misunderstood. "I'm sorry? What?"

"Henry is now old enough to begin drawing from his trust fund. However, I placed a stipulation on it. He must marry a woman of my choosing or he receives nothing. I approved of you."

Fiona stopped short, almost tripping on her own feet. She knew her mouth was hanging open. This was so unexpected she couldn't process what Agatha was saying.

"Are you still there?"

"What? Oh yes. I'm here. You approve of me? For your son? When have you *ever* approved of me? The entire time I was with Hank, you hated everything about me."

"Yes, well, I have met many of the woman my son thinks appropriate, and I realized my mistake. You were the best of the lot."

Fiona began to laugh. "Do you know *why* I broke up with Hank, Agatha?"

"I do not. I told him to go fix things with you and marry you, especially if he ever wanted a penny of his trust fund."

Fiona chuckled again. "I left Hank because I caught him cheating with the maid."

There was silence on the end of the line. Agatha asked, "And?"

"And what? I caught him cheating after we were engaged to be married, Agatha. I found out there were others. If he was doing that before we were married, he would certainly continue after."

"Yes, well. We women must look the other way. Men have needs and cannot always..."

"Stop. Stop right there." Fiona interrupted with fire in her voice. "That might be the life *you* chose, but that isn't the life I want to live. I want a man who, when he commits to being with me and only me for the rest of his life, he means it. I want a man who, when he tells me he is going to be some place, I can trust that he will be there. I want a man who loves me more than any other woman or experience he could have. I don't think that's too much to ask."

"That is not how the world works. We women must simply accept our lot in life."

"Not me, Agatha. Never me."

Fiona hung up the phone. She'd found what she was looking for. She smiled as an idea formed.

Chapter 41

♥

P eter gazed out over the congregation and smiled. There wasn't much he enjoyed more than teaching on a Sunday morning. The Lord had been so good to him lately now that things were back the way they were intended to be.

The last few weeks had been full of changes. Good changes but changes all the same. The two new elders had been installed. Two weeks ago, the congregation had affirmed the decision to add Drew and Joshua to the elder board. Peter was thankful for the additional help. The men were fitting in well. Peter already saw the results of their help in his life.

The worship team took the stage to close out the service. Peter walked quietly to the back, to stand by the door, ready to greet people as they left. He nodded to Manny as they passed.

His brother had moved out just yesterday. He was now living in town, over the hardware store. Having Manny in Haven was a huge help. His younger brother had even taken Todd's place on the worship team.

He liked having all his brothers in Haven. Manny was going to help run Drew's business for him after Kate had the baby.

And their younger brother was even considering setting up a design side for it as well.

Peter chuckled at remembering Manny's run-in with Mrs. Johnson. They'd been hauling a couch up to Manny's apartment when the old woman had pulled up to the curb.

Putting down her window, she'd yelled out, "What is going on here?"

Manny had wiped the sweat out of his eyes with the back of his hand. He stepped closer to the door of her vehicle and said, "Just moving in, ma'am."

"Who are you? I haven't seen you around."

"Manny Grant, ma'am. Nice to meet you."

"What kind of name is that?" Mrs. Johnson had wrinkled her nose at Manny.

"Well, it's mine, ma'am."

"What is it short for?"

Manny sighed. He disliked his full name and rarely used it.

"Well?" Mrs. Johnson tapped a finger on the steering wheel. "Answer me!"

Manny had glanced at where Peter, Drew, and Lucas were standing. The three men all raised eyebrows at him and nodded to Mrs. Johnson. After all, they'd all been raised to respect their elders.

Sighing once more, Manny said, "Emmanuel."

"Well then, that is what I shall call you. Nice to meet you, Emmanuel Grant. That's just what Haven needs, another Grant man around."

She'd put the vehicle into gear and, without looking, pulled away with squealing tires.

"Was she serious?" Lucas asked.

"Since when did Mrs. Johnson use manners?" Drew added.

The three older brothers had laughed and gotten back to work.

Now, Peter caught Fiona's eye from where he was standing off to the side. She gave him a wide smile as the band was finishing up the last song. She'd told him she couldn't spend the afternoon with him today, and he was a little disappointed. There was nothing he loved better than spending Sunday afternoons with Fee.

She was a bit vague about what she needed to do, just, "I can't today." He accepted it, but knew he'd be making a few extra stops at Seascapes with coffee and baked goods throughout the week in hopes of seeing her.

That's all he wanted to do these days. Spend time with Fiona. Now that the note mystery was solved, and he had more help around the church, he thought it might be time. Time to take their relationship to the next level. His stomach gave a little lurch at the thought, but he couldn't stop the wide smile that crossed his face.

He tried to stay engaged with each person as they left, but his thoughts kept wandering back to a certain redhead. He glanced around to see where she was, but he couldn't spot her. Then Mrs. Johnson was standing in front of him.

"Young man, I'm glad to see you came to your senses. I think Joshua and Drew will make excellent elders. Now, what have you heard about poor Leeann?"

Peter held back a grin. Mrs. Johnson had been scandalized over Leeann and her actions. However, Fiona's words on the day of Leeann's arrest, seemed to have found a place in Mrs. Johnson's heart. The older woman had been putting together a contingent of volunteers from the auxiliary to visit Leeann. She wanted to ensure Leeann knew she wasn't alone.

"I think you've likely heard more than I, Mrs. Johnson. I heard you took her under your wing."

"Well, I don't want to boast or anything."

"Then boast in the Lord, Mrs. Johnson. Boast in Him."

"Yes, yes of course. She's doing well. As well as can be expected locked up in that horrible place. I made a point of speaking to the warden on my last visit. I have some ideas on how to make things a little better for all those poor women in there."

Peter couldn't help it. He laughed. He could just picture Mrs. Johnson telling the warden at the state prison how to run things.

"That's wonderful, Mrs. Johnson. That's the way to be Jesus's hands and feet. Now, I need to speak to Mr. Jefferies here. I'll see you later this week, I'm sure."

Before she could say anything else, Peter moved on to the next person in line. He was still grinning over the image he had formed of Mrs. Johnson and the warden.

Soon, all the people had left, and his Sunday was over.

Smiling, he locked the doors before heading to his office to gather his things. Even if Fiona wasn't with him, he thought a walk on the beach was just what he needed on this warm early summer day. May had arrived with fluffy white clouds and warm breezes.

He grabbed the notes he was making for a series he was currently working on and stopped cold. Sitting in the middle of his desk, with his keys on top, was an envelope with his name written in block letters.

He cautiously approached his desk. Leeann had left the notes, so how could there be another one on his desk? Leeann was still sitting in prison. He'd just spoken of it with Mrs. Johnson.

He shook his head and let out a puff of air. No, he was being silly. There was no way Leeann could have left the note. He picked it up and slid the flap of the envelope open. Pulling out the paper, he read the short note.

MEET ME WHERE WE
ATE PIES FOR MY BIRTHDAY.
~FEE

Peter's grin split across his face. He was going to get to see Fee today after all. Snatching up his keys, and leaving the note behind, he practically ran out the door to his truck.

He started his truck and threw it into gear. He tried not to spin his tires on the way out of the parking lot. He was, after all, the pastor. He needed to set an example, like Lucas had told him, but he pushed the speed limit as fast as he dared.

Chapter 42

♥

F iona sat on the boulder near Haven Light with her legs drawn up, her arms wrapped around them, resting her head on her knees. She was praying as she waited for Peter to arrive.

"Lord, thank You for all You've done for me. You have brought me the desire of my heart. You have healed the hurt places inside and brought me new joy with Peter. You didn't have to but thank You for doing so. Please be with Peter as he reads my note. Be with us throughout this relationship. If it's Your will that I do what I'm planning, make it obvious to me."

The waves crashed splashing spray upwards just missing her. She watched seagulls floating up and down on the drafts of air, held up by something unseen. "Lord, that's what it's like with You isn't it? You hold me up, but I can't see You. It doesn't matter because You're there, just like the wind for those birds."

"Like a still, small voice."

Startled, Fiona turned to see Peter standing behind her, hands in his pockets. The wind tousled his dark hair. She wanted to run her fingers through his hair and be the one to tousle it. She laughed as she realized she was jealous of the wind.

"What still, small voice?" She asked as she held out a hand to him. "Come sit with me."

"I couldn't help but overhear that last bit you said, 'wind for the birds.'" Peter settled on the rock next to her. "In the story of Elijah in 1 Kings, he has an encounter with God. Elijah looks for Him in all the things that happens. God sent a storm, an earthquake, and even a fire, but God wasn't in any of those things. He came to Elijah as a whisper or a still, small voice.

"I think we forget sometimes to listen for that voice. We think God is going to speak to us through some major event. But really, it's in those moments when we feel a confirmation, a nudge, a still, small voice saying, 'yes.'"

The wind was whipping Fiona's curly hair all around her. She caught her breath when Peter reached out and tried to tuck some of it behind her ear. Fiona laughed at his attempts. "It's hopeless. I should have brought a hair tie."

"Fiona, you're wonderful. Have I ever told you that?"

"I think you're wonderful, too. I see you got my note?"

"Note? What note? I just happened to see you sitting on the rocks and thought I'd join you." Peter leaned over and nudged her shoulder with his as he laughed.

"You know, lying is a sin. You should be setting a better example than that."

"So I hear!" Peter laughed harder. "I'll need your help with that. You seem to bring out something in me. You make me a better person. I like it."

"Walk with me?" Fiona stood, brushing off the seat of her jeans. She slipped her feet back into her sandals and reached out a hand to Peter. She felt a jolt of pleasure shoot up her arm as his hand grasped hers. Butterflies came to life in her stomach. He had no idea what she was planning. Her heart picked up speed with the anticipation.

She tugged his hand to follow her as they began to pick their way down the nearby trail to the beach. Peter moved ahead and helped her climb down the boulders.

"Such a gentleman," she winked at him.

Laughing, he picked her up around the waist and lifted her down the last boulder to stand in front of him.

"Thank you," she breathed out.

"My pleasure."

The couple walked along the beach, hand in hand. Out of habit, Fiona began scanning the sand for bits of sea glass. The beach along here usually had a few pieces. A sparkle of white caught her eye.

Quickly stooping, she picked up the piece of sea glass. It was as big as the pinkie nail on her hand. She brushed the sand off and examined it. It was smooth and opaque. It was perfect.

"What will you make out of that?" Peter nodded towards the piece of glass in her hand.

Fiona smiled. She couldn't have planned this better if she'd tried. *Thank you, Lord.*

She spoke, "A necklace, I think. A special one."

"A special one? How so?" Peter tugged on her hand to get them walking again, but Fiona pulled her hand away, turning to face him.

"A wedding necklace." Fiona reached into her back pocket and pulled out a folded piece of paper. "Here, read this."

Peter opened the note. She wanted to keep it simple.

I LOVE YOU WITH ALL OF MY HEART.

Peter's smile grew as he read the words. When he looked at her, she dropped to her knees in front of him and took his hand. "Peter Michael Grant, I love you. I love you so much. I want to spend the rest of my life with you. Will you marry me?"

Fiona held her breath. She thought Peter felt the same, but they'd never discussed it. Early on he'd told her he wasn't dating to date but dating with a purpose. What if he said no? She wasn't sure what she would do, but she would have to leave Haven. She couldn't face him day after day if he said no.

She couldn't even believe she'd decided to do this. She'd never even asked a man out. Now here she was asking a man to marry her.

Peter tugged her back to a standing position. Fiona's heart sank. He had such a serious look on his face. "Fee, I don't think this is how it's supposed to be done. I think..." His voice trailed off as he lowered himself to one knee, holding her hand.

"Fiona Ava Gilliam, I love that your personality is larger than life. I love that you have strong opinions, and you aren't afraid to share them. I love that you are a fierce friend and protector of those you love. I love your red hair and your green eyes. I love you, more than I ever imagined was possible."

Peter paused to pull a small jewelry box out of his front pocket. He never let go of Fiona's hand but used his thumb to flip the top open. Turning the box towards her, he held it up. It contained a single marquis cut diamond ring. "And while I love that you asked me first, let me still ask you. Will you marry me?"

Fiona began to laugh even as she felt the tears starting to fall. She held out her hand to him.

Peter pulled the ring out of the box, letting the empty container fall to the sand. He slipped the ring on Fiona's finger. She grabbed his arm, yanking him up.

"Forgive me for being impatient." She looped her arms around his shoulders.

Peter laughed as he leaned towards her. "You still haven't answered my question."

"Yes, absolutely yes."

Peter smiled and closed the distance between them. "I'm so glad you're in my life, Fee." He reached a thumb to wipe a tear off her cheek.

Fiona closed her eyes as Peter's lips settled on hers. Her heart leapt at the thought of not only being Peter's wife, but now she would be sisters with Kate and Bree as well. When God answered her prayer, He certainly went above and beyond.

Fiona tightened her arms around Peter's shoulder, pulling him closer as he deepened the kiss. It had been worth the wait.

Epilogue

♥

Three months later

*C**ome see your new niece. She's adorable and wants to meet her auntie.*

The text Fiona received early this morning now had her hurrying through the front doors of the hospital. She punched the up button on the elevator three times in rapid succession. She'd been praying for months for this day, and that it would be a happy one. She would soon find out if her prayers had been answered.

It had been three months since that day on the beach. Three months since Fiona proposed to Peter only to have him turn around and propose to her. She was still giddy at times over the fact she would be Mrs. Peter Grant in just a few short months. They were going to have a fall wedding at Haven Light. October couldn't get here fast enough.

"C'mon!" Fiona muttered, trying to hurry the elevator. As she reached to hit the button again, she heard a ding and the doors swished open. Stepping in, she punched the button for maternity, bouncing on her toes with excitement.

Kate hadn't answered any of her questions about the baby since she'd sent the first text. Fiona still didn't know if the little one was fighting for her life or if God had made her whole.

The church had been praying for the littlest Grant to arrive safely. At Kate's last ultrasound appointment, just a few weeks before the baby was due, the doctor's hadn't been as certain about the defect. Yet, none of them would admit it might be gone.

When that news had spread, prayer started coming fast and furious that the baby would be born whole. Now, Fiona moved just short of a run down the hallway towards the obstetrics floor. Even if she would only see her niece for a short while before she went to be with Jesus, it would have to be enough.

Fiona just prayed she could be of some comfort to Kate and Drew if tragedy awaited them. No one had wanted to get their hopes up, but Peter had just said last night, "We serve a God of hope. Why shouldn't we hope? He's a God of miracles as well, and I believe He can heal this baby. And if He doesn't heal the baby on this side of heaven, He will certainly heal it on the other side."

Fiona hadn't wanted to hear that. No one really did. She would find out soon enough what God had decided to do.

Knocking lightly on the door, Fiona stuck her head in. "Hey." She stepped fully in, stopping.

Kate was smiling, but Fiona could see she'd been crying recently. Drew was hovering nearby. Her friend was holding a blanket wrapped bundle.

"Is...is she okay?" Fiona's voice cracked. She felt tears welling in her eyes. *Please God, don't take this baby from them.*

"Come on over. Lori wants to meet her Auntie Fee."

Fiona let out a whoosh of air as tears filled her eyes. Kate still hadn't answered her. She hurried to the bedside and leaned over opposite Drew to stare into the face of the new little life.

"Ohhh...she's beautiful." Fiona reached out a tentative finger and stroked the small cheek. The baby was sleeping, but one side of her mouth tipped up in a half smile at the touch.

"And her heart?" Fiona couldn't tear her eyes from the baby. Such softness. Such newness. An unmarred life.

"It's perfect."

Fiona's head snapped up. "What?"

"Fee, God fixed her heart. God fixed my baby's heart. There's no evidence of any defect. They had her in tests most of the morning. Poor thing is worn out. They couldn't find any scrap of evidence of anything. Her heart is perfect."

Tears really did start to pour at that news. Fiona's hand covered her mouth. She smiled through the tears. "Kate. I...I don't know what to say."

"God is good."

"Yes, yes He is." Fiona leaned in to hug Kate, squashing the baby slightly between them. Fiona stepped back and turned her gaze once more to baby Lori in Kate's arms.

Behind Fiona, she heard the door open, and a familiar voice ask, "Is it okay to come in?"

She spun and hurried to greet Peter, pulling him in through the door. "Come meet your niece. Our niece. She's beautiful, Peter. Absolutely beautiful. And she's whole. Her heart is whole."

Fiona saw relief wash over Peter's face.

"Thank you, Lord!" Peter walked over to give Drew a hug before coming to stand beside Fiona.

"Oh! What's her full name?" Fiona was eager to have a name for the sweet face.

"Her name is Lori Hannah Grant. Lori for my sister. It means 'grace.' Then Hannah, which means 'gift of God's favor.' God has granted us His grace and favor by giving us this sweet baby girl, whole and healed."

All four adults simply stared at the baby sleeping in her mother's arms.

Unafraid. Complete. Healed. God still worked miracles. Fiona was currently watching one sleep.

"Do you think you'd like one of those someday?" Peter leaned close to whisper in Fiona's ear, making shivers go down her arms.

"Absolutely. As many as God will gift us." Fiona smiled at him. God had granted her the desires of her heart. She would soon be a wife. She prayed not long after she would be a mother. God was truly good.

Delight yourself in the Lord;
and He will give you the desires of your heart.
Psalm 37:4

Thank You

I hope you enjoyed finally seeing the culmination of Peter and Fiona's relationship that began back in book one of the Haven series, *Seascapes*. I certainly had a lot of fun writing it. If you enjoyed it (and even if you didn't), please consider leaving a review or stars on your favorite review platform. Reviews help others decide if they would also like to read my offerings to the book world.

If you enjoyed this story, you may also like *Saltwater Orchard*. It's set before *Seascapes* and features two of the very minor characters from the Haven series. Sign up for my newsletter by scanning the QR code below to get a free digital copy of the story.

Ryann has been a single mom for seven years. Life has taken some unexpected turns and when she finds herself with the prospect of either living out of her car or squatting in an empty barn, she opts for the barn. Not realizing the new owner is someone from her past.

Richard thought he was on the fast track to become a vice-president of Central Bank. His girlfriend had his life all planned out. Until he finds out his uncle left Richard his apple orchard. He hadn't planned on moving to Haven, but at the prospect of the farm being using for fire training, he had no choice. He heads to the small town to try to reclaim the farm and make it profitable. And on his first night there, he discovers something unexpected.

Will Ryann and Richard be able to move forward instead of being stuck in the past? Can they trust God with not only their life but with their hearts?

I love connecting with readers!

- evelyngrace@evelyngracebooks.com.

- www.facebook.com/evelyngracebooks

- www.evelyngracebooks.com

Acknowledgments

I can do all things through Him who strengthens me.
~Philippians 4:13

I'm now a little further into this writing career. I'm still finding it hard and difficult but also wonderful. The encouragement I continue to receive makes me want to continue on. Thank you to all who ask me who things are going. It helps!

I want to thank my hubby. He's still the best beta reader I have. The feedback he gives me either makes me laugh, sigh, or roll of my eyes. But it all makes the story better.

Thank you to my fabulous sister, Beth, and my wonderful friend, Emma, both of whom read the story again after I made some major changes. They assured me the changes all made it better! And Emma gets an extra shout out because this lovely, homeschooled teen wrote me a full book report! I'm still in awe. She used graphics, quotes…it was fabulous! I'm a "words of encouragement" person so I held it all dearly in my heart.

Thank you to my friend, Robin. Your encouragement to "just get it done" constantly rings in my ears. The writing sprints and cactus chicken help as well. And they always makes writing time fly by.

And last, but certainly not least in any way is my Lord and Savior, Jesus Christ. I am a new creation because of my relationship with Him. Thank You for helping me with each story. I pray they continue to bring glory to You first and foremost.